CB

P9-AOQ-495

She was alone again . . .

And yet she was not alone. The dark stranger squeezed back into the narrow, sandy crevice behind her, wrapped once around in his blanket, and fell asleep instantly. she could not see him. He made no sound. Still, she felt his comforting presence. She might be lost in this forbidding wilderness, but he seemed right at home. He could find dry firewood in a rain-drenched desert. He knew what to do and was bold enough to do it. Under the rudest of conditions he had effortlessly prepared a complete and filling meal. His strength was sufficient for them both. All admirable qualities in a man.

She twisted around to look at him. His face was completely relaxed, his breathing deep and even. He surely did not look like any heaven-sent ambassador. On closer scrutiny she saw him as a gangling, over-grown boy, a man-child who had matured into adulthood without leaving behind the essence of childhood. He could not possibly be as innocent as his sleeping face suggested. Fascinating.

Before she fell asleep, Naomi would again address her heavenly Father. She must thank Him for His providence. Yes, the arrival of this vulgar stranger was providential. She turned to study him again.

She did not even know his name.

SUMMER SNOW

Sandy Dengler

Serenade/Saga
BOOKS

of the Zondervan Publishing House
Grand Rapids, Michigan

SUMMER SNOW
Copyright © 1984 by The Zondervan Corporation,
1415 Lake Drive, S.E.,
Grand Rapids, Michigan 49506

Library of Congress Cataloging in Publication Data

Dengler, Sandy
    Summer snow.

    I. Title.
PS3554.E524S9   1983   813'.54   83-21667
ISBN 0-310-46432-3

Edited by Anne Severance and Janet Wilson
Designed by Kim Koning

All rights reserved. No part of this publication may be reproduced, stored in a retrieval system, or transmitted in any form or by any means—electronic, mechanical, photocopy, recording, or any other—except for brief quotations in printed reviews, without the prior permission of the publisher.

Printed in the United States of America

85 86 87 88 89 / 8 7 6 5 4 3 2

CHAPTER 1

EVERYONE KNOWS DESERTS are hot and dry. Naomi Morrison pondered this universal knowledge as she sat on a rain-slick rock, her teeth chattering. The rain pounded its icy fists against her wool cape. The frigid moisture penetrated relentlessly; she could feel its wetness across her shoulders.

Everyone knows deserts are vast, silent expanses of shimmering scenery, with muted colors which change with the shifting light. However, Naomi squinted in vain, watching, but the swirling, misty rain turned color to gray and obscured vision beyond a mile or so. She listened for creaking and rattling and horses' feet. The stagecoach driver had promised to return for her promptly. That was hours ago. Where could they have gone? Surely they had not forgotten her out here along the road.

Everyone knows deserts are uninhabited, that in a desert you are alone. Everyone was right on that point. She was absolutely the only person in the world.

To keep her mind off her peril, Naomi pictured what she would do as soon as she reached San Francisco. First, she

5

would wash her hair and arrange it properly. She could sit on her hair when it hung loose, but for the past ten days she had not let it down. It must be filthy by now. It probably didn't even look brown any more.

Then, clean and business-like again, she would march straight into the main office of Wells, Fargo and Company. She would tell the president (or general manager or whomever) in no uncertain terms that one of his drivers had abandoned her in the middle—the very middle—of Arizona territory. It was certainly not to Wells Fargo's credit that she had reached San Francisco at all. Were she not a plucky woman who could make her own way, her bones would now be bleaching in the Arizona sun. Surely some sort of refund was in order. Naomi smiled. Just imagining that scene gave her a certain measure of comfort.

Perhaps she should begin walking west. The driver had told her to wait, but she was getting so cold.

Directly behind her a horse sneezed. Naomi bolted straight up and spun around. Six feet away, an immense horse face stared placidly into hers. She yelped, more in surprise than in fear. Her eyes darted up to the rider, and she took a nervous step backward.

Was he an Indian? Surely so. But then again, perhaps not. Local Indians wore their hair long and pulled back in a honcho knot tied with white yarn. This man's hair ended around his ears. Was it black, or was it actually brown turned black by the rain-wetness? She decided it was brownish-black. Most Indians Naomi knew were rather short and square-built. This fellow must tower over six feet tall. Lanky legs hung slack in the stirrups, and his long arms folded casually across his saddle fork. Dungaree cuffs crept out from under heavy leather chaps. His thick sheepskin coat looked so thoroughly oiled that it must be nearly water-proof. He was certainly dressed for the weather.

6

He smiled pleasantly. "May I be of service, ma'am?" There was no trace of accent in his voice, no hint of guttural Indian gibberish or incorrect pronunciation. Perhaps he was not an Indian after all. Still, either his skin was deeply sun-tanned or . . .

"I, ah, no. No, I think not. Th-thank you. My driver will be returning m-m-momentarily."

"Don't think I'd count on it."

"He said he would. I have n-n-no reason to doubt. He has p-problems with his mules. He calls them green b-b-broke. I c-c-c-call them obstreperous. B-but he'll be back."

"May I ask why you were left behind?"

His question was mildly embarrassing, though he surely did not realize it. "We were, ah, engaged in a comfort stop when his m-m-m-mules bolted. I don't know why. B-but away they w-went. You may go on. Th-thank you." Why was she stuttering so? He had startled her, but she certainly was not *that* frightened—or was she? He loomed so tall, so dark, so ominous. And she was essentially at his mercy out here.

His lips tightened, perhaps a gesture of thoughtfulness. He shook his head. "You've been sitting here over three hours. I doubt . . ."

"How do you p-p-presume to know that?"

"Because I've been watching you that long, and I have no idea how long you sat here before I noticed you. Your mud wagon must have wrecked—especially likely if his mules weren't well broke. They'd have been here if they were going to get back by dark. The road's empty now. No one out there."

"I ap-p-p-preciate your concern, but I'll get on just fine. G-G-G-Good day, s-sir." With a shudder she remembered the panic in the departing driver's voice as he called to her to stay put. His mules were completely out of control then, and the stagecoach (actually a mud wagon; this stranger was right) was so old, it groaned and creaked at every turn of the wheels.

Naomi studied the man who stood before her. On second thought, he must be an Indian. Any civilized man would have recognized her greeting as a request to leave. However, neither he nor his huge horse moved. What color was his horse anyway? She had never seen one quite that shade before. Tinges of blue and charcoal gray made it the color of finely tempered blue steel. Black knees and white feet set it off smartly, as did an even white blaze down its face. It was a lovely animal.

Very well, if he would not leave, she would. She dipped her head good day, turned her back on him and started walking. She staggered slightly. Somewhat chagrined, she squared her shoulders and marched off westward. She should have done this hours ago instead of sitting about like a dumb bump. A few hundred yards down the road, she glanced back surreptitiously. Neither man nor horse had moved an inch.

The road wound around a low and sandy hill. She tried to miss the puddles in its ruts, but her feet got wet anyway. She pulled her dark cape closer around. She couldn't stop shivering.

She had thought to pray when first her transportation had clattered away down the road without her. She now considered the value of more earnest petition. The man behind her was lost from view and the road ahead stretched on desolate forever. She folded stiffly to her knees and clasped her hands in an attitude of prayer. She addressed her Father on her own behalf and on behalf of the driver. She added a precautionary request for protection against any marauding Indians. And, though she was cold and uncomfortable, she was also safe—at least thus far. She thanked Him for that.

Her legs were even stiffer as she lurched to her feet. Not only was the hem of her skirts soaked, now the front was also. She brushed off her dark traveling dress as much as she could and continued on. She should be warming up from this brisk exercise. Instead, she felt colder.

Now the road tipped sharply downward to what normally might have been a little stream. But today it coursed, brown and riffly, a good thirty feet wide. She thought briefly of flashfloods, but flashflooding was not supposed to occur during these slow and steady winter rains. Winter? Wasn't it time for spring? The weather certainly didn't feel like it.

The road disappeared into the gurgling water. This may well be why the driver wanted her to wait. How deep was it? Since there was no recourse but to wade across, she would do so, though carefully. Her shoes were wet already; now they would be thoroughly soaked. Gingerly she took one step out into the water, then another. Instantly the raw cold permeated. Her toes, once blissfully numb, began to ache. She sloshed across the stream in agony, trying in vain to keep her skirts out of the frigid water. She closed her eyes and bore onward. It was much farther across than she would have expected.

How long did she continue walking, and where was that driver? Except for the constant hissing patter of the rain, she heard nothing. The road had become little more than a path. And now it disappeared completely. She stopped. Scratchy little bushes crowded around her shins. Rocks studded hillsides to her left and her right. No stagecoach could negotiate this chaotic wilderness. How could she have lost something as large and obvious as a major road? It must have happened when she forded the stream. Yes, that was it. The road turned and she did not, for the swirling water had obscured the curve. Or perhaps she had angled wrongly across the stream. She could see better from atop that little hill right there. She would observe precisely where she had gone wrong and retrace her way.

Stumbling, she slogged to the top of the rise. There she saw other rises, all equally high. She distinguished nothing remotely like a road or track or fence or farm—no hint of which way west might lie. Surely she was only a few yards off the track. Perhaps she should simply go back. But which way was that?

Suddenly, quite unexpectedly, pure abject terror engulfed her. Never in all her twenty-three years had she felt so hideously, horribly fear-struck. Lost! And it was all her own foolishness which had brought her here. To complicate matters she was exceedingly angry with herself. Why had she not stayed put on that rock? Surely she would have been rescued by now; it was nearly dark. Her anger burned even more fiercely against that stubborn, ignorant Indian. If he had left her when he was supposed to, she would not have started walking. If he had been the least bit reassuring about the stagecoach, she would have waited patiently.

The terror and anger boiled together into a consuming, fiery rage. She felt like hiking up her sodden skirts and just running, but she was too cold, too stiff, to move. She felt like screaming. Now there was a fine idea! She opened her mouth, but her anguished cry was more a chilly little croak.

Darkness was closing her in now, dragged down around her ears by the swirling rain. It must not come so soon; it would conceal her from her rescuers! It cut her off from everything safe and warm and civilized. She took a deep, shuddering breath. She had been forgetting her Father, her Rock, her Strength. She must discipline her mind. She must restore some semblance of order to her thoughts. Her reason whirled as wildly as the rain.

Hoofbeats clattered on the stones behind her. A horse was scrambling up this hill to her; she was saved! They had

10

heard her pitiful little cry and come to get her.

No, they had not. It was he, the object of her fury. The lanky Indian rode up beside her and swooped down out of his saddle. He stood squarely in front of her.

His voice was strong and steady. "Do you know how late it is?"

"S-s-s-certainly. A-A-A-ril twennnny-ssssix, eight-eight-eighteen eighty-n-n-nine. M-M-M-Mon . . ."

"It's nearly dark. If you think you're lost now, just wait five minutes. You won't be able to see your toes. I doubt you can feel 'em now. No moon, overcast . . ."

"I am n-n-not losht." Her lips were tight as wood and her tongue so sluggish it would form no words.

He was frowning at her. "You're freezing."

"N-n-nons . . ."

He grimaced, worried. This Indian—or whatever he was—acted genuinely concerned. She was especially taken by the way his face flexed and changed with his changing thoughts. It was a very expressive face and, were she looking at it objectively under different circumstances, quite a handsome one.

Whatever made him think one could freeze in Arizona? On a desert? When it wasn't even snowing or making icicles or anything of the sort? She remembered licking icicles from the porch roof when she was a child in Ohio. She was nowhere near freezing then. She remembered how her little woolen mittens would adhere to the ice and leave behind tiny, curly bits of hair.

He moved so quickly she could not begin to defend herself. He wrapped long serpentine arms around her and dragged her forward. She tried to struggle, but he literally swept her off her feet, heels over head. The inside of her right leg clunked against his saddle. He shoved upward. She grabbed at the saddle to keep from falling, but her fingers

11

would not tighten. His hand wrapped firmly around her leg just above the knee and held her in place. He might be preventing her from falling, but no gentleman would dream of touching a lady *there* regardless of the circumstance. Obviously he was no gentleman. Of all the brazen, impudent . . . She knew she was now seated in his saddle, but she felt disoriented. And now he swung up behind her.

He handled his horse with his right hand, his left arm wrapped around her shoulders. She was anchored snugly and securely in the one place she absolutely did *not* want to be. Struggling was ineffectual; she learned that quickly enough. Intensely wearied, she drooped back against his bulk.

"No." His voice rumbled, distant. "Keep fighting. Keep moving. It'll help."

She was so cold now that she did not really feel chilled. She had heard somewhere that when you feel all warm and sleepy like this, you are one step short of dying. Perhaps he was right, and she really was freezing.

The raindrops stopped pelting her cheeks, though they still came. They touched gently, feather-light, here and there. They drifted through the swarming darkness.

Despite any earlier danger, she abhorred the thought of being carried off by some semi-savage. The rescuers from the coach stop would never find her now. Oh, if only she had stayed at her place on the road! She was in danger then, but much more so now.

"I f-f-feel like I'm j-j-j-j-jumping out of the f-frying p-p-pan into the . . . the f-f-fire."

"You can use a little fire just now, ma'am." He leaned forward against her. His horse scrambled uphill, then jolted downhill.

A fluffy blob clung to her lower lashes and melted into her eye. "Thisss izzz s-snow."

"Yep."

She tried to ask "Where are you taking me?" but it wouldn't come out right. Huge snowflakes fluttered around her face. She could not feel them touch, nor could she see them beyond a foot or so in the darkness.

He seemed to understand her garbled question. "Shelter. I was gonna give you a ride to the stage stop, or maybe to Leupp. But they're too far away. You're too cold. I'll warm you up and then worry what to do with you."

He talked as if she were a child or some inanimate object. It irritated her in an abstract, distant way. Everything seemed abstract and distant, in fact. Her discomfort, her present circumstance, her very soul and feelings seemed to dissolve into the wet night air. She became a phantasm, some sort of diffuse spirit observing the corporeal self from afar. She floated. Despite the constant jouncing, she drifted in and out of sleep.

Was she dying? Perhaps. This morning at breakfast, her only meal today, she would have fought fiercely against the prospect of death. She did not welcome it with open arms now, but neither did she resist. God was distant. Life was distant. She could feel neither of them.

And she did not care.

CHAPTER 2

SHE BOBBED. SHE jiggled. Then the jarring stopped. She hung suspended, utterly alone. He had abandoned her atop his horse. She sat swaying in the emptiness. She called out and could not understand the sounds her mouth made. She felt herself sliding. He dragged her down, pulled at her, scooped her against him. She despised being mauled and tossed about like a haunch of beef.

A dull orange glow flickered in front of her. It took her some moments to realize she was sitting in a soggy little pile, her legs folded beneath her. His face floated, disembodied, in the darkness beyond. He dumped a huge, loose wad of something dark upon his fledgling fire. The flames sputtered, angry at having been fed such unappetizing fare, then crackled high and bright. His face glowed in the new light. He glanced at her frequently and anxiously as he coaxed his little fire into a roaring blaze.

Mesmerized by the nervous, wavering flames, she drifted toward sleep. He was tugging at her cape. Instinctively she tugged back. She tried to clutch it close around her, but it ripped out of her fingers. And now he was unbuttoning her dress down the back! Oh, no! The very worst imaginable thing was happening and she was too numb, too muddled to resist adequately.

He seized her by both shoulders and twisted her around, the better to meet her eye to eye. "Listen. Can you hear me? You're soaked to the skin. Your dress has to come off or you'll never warm up." He shook her again. "Do you hear? Just the top half. We'll let the skirts go for now. You're safe. You can trust me. Do you understand?"

She tried to respond but her mouth made incoherent noises. No, she did not trust him. She did not trust him the slightest bit, but she could not articulate her fears. He twisted her around again to face away from him and peeled the dress down off her shoulders. Not content with that indignity, he was stripping off her cotton chemise as well! The effrontery of this brute!

He remained behind her. Certainly, he could not see much, even if he chose to leer. Still . . . She expected shame to wash her face in a hot blush, but she was too cold for that. In fact, she felt very nearly past caring what the lout did. She should, however, at least say something.

As she turned her head to speak to him, she saw that he was taking his own heavy coat off. Yes, the worst was indeed about to happen. She sat in a cramped little cave or overhang of some sort, lost beyond hope of rescue, and now this craven beast would have his way with her. All these years she had been so careful to maintain a respectable distance from men. She had kept herself undefiled, not just for the sake of propriety, but because she understood clearly what God wanted and expected from His own, and she would respect His wishes. But now this . . .

The bulky sheepskin coat fell across her bare shoulders, so heavy it nearly toppled her. Ah, it was marvelously cozy from his body heat. He swaddled her in its snug, fluffy warmth.

Over the coals at one side he made coffee in a blackened porcelain-fleck pot. He offered her some in a tin mug, but her fingers would not grasp the cup, much less loop through the handle. Gently he molded her hands around the hot mug with his own warm hands. He steadied the cup as she sipped. The heat from the tin stabbed into her fingers. She felt the scalding coffee glide clear down to her stomach. Normally she disdained coffee, but he had laced this brew liberally with sugar. When he asked "More?" she managed a vigorous nod.

The fire fizzled and waned.

He knelt beside her and gently tipped her face toward his. "Can you hear me? Listen. I'm going to unsaddle and scrounge some more wood. I want you to lie down and stay there, hear? Don't want you falling into the fire if you drift off asleep." He studied her intently. "Hear me?" Apparently it was not a rhetorical question. He repeated it. "Hear me?"

She nodded. He tipped her onto her side beside the coals. His blue cambric shirt disappeared into the outer darkness.

He returned with a small boldly striped blanket. "My saddle blanket here is good and warm. Let's wrap your legs in it." Before she could move he flicked her skirts to just above her knees and tucked the hot, scratchy wool around her. He was gone again.

How many hours did she lie beside that smoky orange fire? She had no way of telling. Her little brooch watch had stopped running weeks ago, probably permanently. It was in her trunk now. But where were her trunks? Buried in a wreck along an isolated road? Sitting in the Flagstaff coach office, luxuriating in warmth she needed here? She could tell this man's ministrations were working. She was begin-

16

ning to thaw. Eventually she had warmed enough to start shivering again. It seemed a curious contradiction in terms, to warm enough to shiver.

She smelled bacon and heard it sizzle. Bacon? She jacked herself back to a sitting position. He grinned at her from across the fire and jiggled a pan in the coals.

"Midnight snack. Want some?"

Apparently he had fried bacon and sliced potato in the same pan and now was stirring in a scrambled egg. Horrid as the combination sounded, it looked and smelled delicious. She nodded.

For the first time she looked around—really observed. She sat toward the back of a four-foot high overhang. The fire was set far enough back under the rock to keep the cave warm but close enough to the open air to spill its smoke out into the thick darkness. The rock all around her was tan and crumbly, the floor beneath her sandy. She could see white dusting on the little bushes in the periphery of firelight. Snow.

She watched the flames jitter across the coals. The warmer she got and the more clearly she could think, the more shame weighed her down. He had stripped her half naked (though to be fair she must remember he had covered her up again promptly). He did not seem to care where he touched her. He had absolutely no sense of decency or consideration. He was so callous he did not even notice his own impropriety. She could not so much as look at him directly. She stared instead at that hot, greasy midnight snack. She did not care to speak at all, certainly not to make trivial conversation. Even as the pain of being chilled abated, she felt utterly miserable.

His eyes, deep and brown, were framed in long, thick lashes. Viewed objectively, his eyes were exceedingly attractive, the perfect complement to the other well-formed

17

features of his face. The eyelids crinkled at the corners when he grinned. "You look better. Diddle your fingers."

She held out a hand and moved her fingers. The stranger joined her in laughter at the attempt. Anyway, her fingers worked again. He gave her a portion of food and a spoon in a tin plate. He used the fork. Just as well—she'd probably put out her eye, or perforate her nose if she tried to eat with a fork just now.

He made more coffee. He baked papery unleavened corn cakes on a hot rock beside the coals.

She drank the coffee, although she much preferred tea. She ate the strange curling little tortillas because she was bidden. After all his effort to cook, decorum required that she sample them. They were remarkably tasty.

He stood up as far as the overhang would permit. He was bent over almost double nonetheless. He must be well over six feet tall. "Try to put down some more coffee and *piki*. If you think you can manage for a while, I'll get some sleep. Been a long night."

"A very long night."

If he noted any irony in her tone of voice, he made no sign. He squeezed back into the narrow, sandy crevice behind her, wrapped once around in his blanket and fell asleep in moments. She was alone again.

And yet she was not alone. She could not see him behind her. He made no sound. Still, she felt his comforting presence. She might be lost in this forbidding wilderness, but he seemed right at home. He could find dry firewood in a rain-drenched desert. He knew what to do and was bold enough to do it. Under the rudest of conditions he had effortlessly prepared a complete and filling meal. His strength was sufficient for them both—comforting attributes in a man.

Before she fell asleep she would again address her

heavenly Father (what strange circumstances in which to say bedtime prayers!). She must thank Him for His providence. Yes, the arrival of this vulgar stranger was providential. She must ask God's continuing help in reaching civilization again; she was determined to reach San Francisco via Flagstaff. But she must earn some more money before the final lap of her journey. Surely there was some sort of honest work in Flagstaff—seamstress, cook, something. By education and profession she was a schoolmistress, but she did not dare hope an opening would await her in a school. Such things never happened this time of year. She might ask around, however. One never knew. She would petition her Father in that matter also. And of course she would thank Him once again for providing His Son. Her present jeopardy aside, He always brought her through. God had saved her soul through His Son and now had saved her physical life through . . .

. . . through this man right here. She twisted around to look at him. His face was completely relaxed, his breathing deep and even. He surely did not look like any heaven-sent ambassador. On closer scrutiny, she saw him as a gangling, overgrown boy, a man-child who had matured into adulthood without leaving behind the essence of childhood. He could not possibly be as innocent as his sleeping face suggested. Fascinating.

She turned back to the fire. No, she much preferred the urbane man, the well-traveled sophisticate, the cultured man of letters. She would marry such a man, Lord willing. Surely San Francisco abounded in them, for it was now a cosmopolitan center of trade and wealth. The thought of San Francisco excited her all over again. After all, it was eighteen hundred and eighty-nine, and the city was booming now that the transcontinental railroad linked it directly to the rest of the country. It offered opportunity unbounded, not just in

19

business and finance but in arts and letters also. She was a teacher, a very good teacher who appreciated the arts. She would surely find herself a comfortable niche in San Francisco.

Would she find a husband also? In a world of bankers, sea captains, railroad builders—and few women—she should have ample choice. She was twenty-three; she should have married years ago. But she would not tie herself to a life of service to a boorish farm boy with the mind to populate the whole Ohio farm country with more boorish farm boys. School had given her the taste of culture. Now she wanted more. She might marry and she might not, but she would at least choose polite society.

However, San Francisco lay far ahead in her future, months away. Her more immediate future contrasted starkly with the city on the bay. To reach that high and distant goal, she must thread her way through this next day and the next and the next. Her present circumstance, and the days to follow, depended largely upon the unpretentious man asleep behind her. She turned to study him again.

She did not even know his name.

CHAPTER 3

"NAME'S ABRAHAM LINCOLN RAWLINS. What's yours?"

"Naomi Morrison." She thought momentarily of adding on a how-do-you-do and abandoned the notion. The situation had progressed much too far for that. Ten feet beyond the overhang, the big gray horse stood munching on a small, gray-green bush. Naomi sat beside the dying embers, tucked her knees up under her skirts, and watched Abraham Lincoln Rawlins saddle his horse. He moved gracefully. His arms flowed from here to there. They extended themselves and tucked in. Long as they were, they never flailed.

Beyond the cover of their rock roof, the ground was soaked. A smattering of snow stuck to grass tufts and bushes and powdered distant buttes. Naomi rejoiced that such distances were visible again. The mist and cloud cover were breaking up, the sun forcing its way out. The snow would disappear quickly now.

How should she address this man? Mr. Rawlins seemed not quite appropriate if he were indeed an Indian (and how

21

does one ask tactfully about ancestry?). Yet for him it sounded natural.

She cleared her throat. "Regarding a term of address."

His eyes twinkled. "Miss Morrison isn't enough?"

"That's fine. I mean for you."

"I hate Abe. Some call me Linc." He flopped his rolled blanket over the back of his saddle and snugged it down. As he turned away, his horse moved forward to reach a tastier-looking bush.

Linc came ambling back up to the overhang and plopped down on the far side of the fire. "Feel all right?"

"Yes. Thank you." She gazed out across the broad wash through crystalline air to the whitened mesas so far away. She loved distance. "Who would think it would snow in the desert?"

"Lots of surprises in the desert." He was studying her.

"Aren't there?" She glanced at him, then quickly averted her eyes. Why should she feel self-conscious around him? Foolishness.

She hauled herself to her feet and stepped out from under the rock roof into a burst of dazzling morning sun. She took a deep breath. Standing out here in the open, she could look at him again. "Where were you bound when you happened upon me? Perhaps we can continue in that direction. You've been sorely inconvenienced already."

"I'm headed up toward Moenkopi."

"You say 'up' north?"

He nodded.

"Mmm. I'm going west. San Francisco, eventually."

"The peaks or the city?"

"What?"

"San Francisco Peaks, or California?"

"California, of course."

He unfolded his lanky frame out into the sun and

22

stretched mightily. "Traveling should be easier for you now. This has gotta be the last snow of the season."

"I certainly hope so." She shook out her cape. It was nearly dry. Her legs ached. The swirling darkness of last night seemed like a bad dream.

The man slung himself effortlessly up into his saddle and reached down to her. She slipped her foot into his stirrup and tried to plan a tasteful and decent way to mount a horse when riding astride. So far as she could figure, there was none. He grabbed not her hand but her upper arm. He dragged straight up and she found herself scrambling to perch on his bedroll. She shifted carefully, settled, and tugged at her skirt; her ankles remained uncovered. Must this journey be punctuated by such indignities?

Linc Rawlins' horse was very much like the man himself —oversized, easy-going and casual. The animal ambled splat-footed out across the wet ground with a smooth and swaying rhythm. The blanket offered a comfortable enough seat, but it lurched precariously. She was forced to keep one hand decorously on his shoulder—and to grip indecorously with both hands now and then.

"What's your horse's name?"

"Nizhoni."

"Oh." She pondered a moment. "An Indian name. Does it mean something that can be translated into English?"

"It means 'pretty.'"

"That's very nice. He is a lovely animal." She glanced nervously at the ground for the hundredth time. "Big. Tall. But lovely. Very pretty."

"Like you."

"What?"

"Nizhoni. You're *nizhoni*."

"Mr. Rawlins . . ."

"Linc."

23

She did not reply. Her cheeks were hot. Up to this moment he had almost been a gentleman. Why did he choose to get personal and spoil the mood? Nizhoni stumbled, throwing her against the broad sheepskin coat. The horse slipped back into his easy, lolling gait. She shifted again, so as not to sit so close to the man.

The morning sun peered over her right shoulder. They were angling more or less to the northwest, but she saw no hint of a road to Flagstaff.

"Ah, Mr. Rawlins . . ."

"Linc."

"Linc. Do you have a specific destination in mind?"

"Mmm-hmm. Perfect place for you."

"San Francisco is the perfect place for me."

"Don't intend to ride that far."

"You said Moko . . . Mono . . . where?"

"Moe-en-KOE-pee. There's a couple Navajo clans there, and some farmers. White settlers. I'm staying south of there."

"Staying. You don't live there permanently, then."

"Don't live anywhere permanently."

"Isn't that somewhat, ah, peripatetic?"

"You're condemning wanderlust, right? You make it sound like a disease."

"I didn't mean to be rude. I don't . . ." She bit her lip.

"You got a touch of it yourself—sitting out there on that rock all alone, fifty miles from the closest peaked roof."

"I'm traveling from Santa Fe. Having a precise origin and a precise destination is hardly peripatetic. I worked in Santa Fe several years as a schoolmistress. Then I decided to move to San Francisco. It's partly ill fortune and partly my own impatience that put me out on that rock. I should have stayed with the railroad train."

"Santa Fe isn't big enough for you?"

"You make *that* sound like a disease. Santa Fe is a charming town. Venerable. Sedate. Elegant."

"Dry, huddled, dull, and everybody speaks Spanish."

"You've been to Santa Fe?"

"Passed through. Ever been over to Bosque Redondo?"

"Fort Sumner area? No." She mulled his question. "Didn't the army intern some Navajo Indians there about a decade ago? No, it was longer ago than that. Then you're Navajo."

"Part. My mother is. Pa was a Hoosier."

"From Indiana! Why, I was born and raised in northeastern Ohio. My father owns a farm near Maumee; that's near Toledo. We were practically next-door neighbors." She stopped. "Wait. How could your father possibly have met your mother in Indiana?"

"I said he was *from* Indiana. A horse soldier with Kit Carson's outfit. He was supposed to chase my mother from Chinle to Fort Sumner on the point of his bayonet—her and eight thousand other Dineh. But he fell in love with her instead. Married her and took her back to this little farm he bought in Kansas." The sheepskin coat under Naomi's hand seemed to heave helplessly. "He died in '73. Last couple years I been looking around for her. Didn't find her."

"When was the last you saw your mother?"

"Spring of '79, when I left home. Figured I was fifteen and didn't need 'er any more. Never realized *she* might need *me.*"

The way his voice dropped indicated that he was finished discussing the matter. Should she pursue the topic further? What he said—and did not say—intrigued her. She was trying to decide how to delicately phrase an inquiry about his Indiana father when he reined Nizhoni in abruptly. She snatched his shoulders with both hands to avoid sliding off.

Half a mile beyond them, three canvas tents perched out

25

on an exposed knob beside the wash. A thin, ragged line of blue smoke drifted up from somewhere within the camp. Downhill of the tents, a man was saddling three horses.

Linc leaned forward. Nizhoni lurched into a flaccid jog, his ears flopping.

"Who is that? I didn't know Indians used tents like that." Naomi bobbed wildly until she could adjust to the jouncy gait.

"Heard about him from some Dineh near Leupp couple weeks ago. I think you'll like 'im. He uses words even longer'n yours. Don't know how peripatetic he is, though." Linc Rawlins was making fun of her. She knew it, even if she couldn't see his face. She imagined those dark eyes dancing with smug delight.

They rode up the broad wash and climbed the hill to the tents. As they approached the camp she recognized the hostler as being Apache, at least in part. He was short and stocky, almost fat. His costume combined an interesting mix of breechclout and chaps, checkered shirt and concho belt. He was also partly Navajo, although he tied his long, blowing hair back from his eyes with the Apache-style ragaround-the-brow. Suspicious and dour, he left the horses and came uphill to stand beside the tents.

A second man, taller than the first, appeared from nowhere. He had abandoned breechclout for dungarees, and his hair was pulled back tightly into a honcho knot—Navajo. He was nowise as tall as Linc, but he approached six feet.

Naomi was about to ask why they were entering so unusual an Indian camp when the obvious owner stepped out of the nearest tent. She took a deep breath. If ever a dream prince were personified, here he stood. Tall and solid, he was built like a Greek god. His tawny hair seemed sunbleached, and his skin was tanned a deep, golden brown.

26

Those huge hazel eyes . . . She very nearly smiled in his face. Whatever his true name, he was Phoebus. Apollo. Master of the Sun.

Best of all, despite these primitive surroundings, he dressed elegantly and properly. Here was a correct gentleman who did not abandon clean shirts and straight ties simply because they might be inconvenient. Even his boots had been recently blacked. And yet there was no hint of foppishness, no suggestion that he might be an ineffectual dandy.

Linc kicked free of one stirrup and twisted aside in the saddle. Naomi stretched out her leg and groped, fumbling for the emptied stirrup. She was starting to slide off her perch too soon. Then Phoebus was there. Strong hands gripped her waist and lowered her gently to the ground. She straightened.

Linc reined Nizhoni aside and away. "Madam." He nodded pleasantly and rode off.

Naomi and the stranger called out "Wait!" simultaneously, but Linc was clattering down the slope and out across the wash. Naomi stood dumbfounded. Of all the crude and ill-mannered things he had done thus far, dumping her summarily on this stranger's doorstep was the worst.

The wash curved west and disappeared beyond a cluster of gaunt gray mesquites. Nizhoni's rump blended into the landscape beyond the trees, and she could see them no more.

He was gone.

CHAPTER 4

EVERYONE KNOWS IT is not proper for a woman to address a man unless they have first been formally introduced. Naomi stood non-plussed, shifting uneasily from foot to foot. But this gentleman's discomfiture must be even greater, for she had come as a complete surprise to him.

She turned to meet those hazel eyes. "Ah, this seems to be an awkward situation not even Lord Chesterfield allowed for. Very well. Circumstance requires that I introduce myself. My name is Naomi Morrison. How do you do?"

"Morrison? Really! You wouldn't by chance be related to the Morrison of Colorado after whom the geologic formation is named?"

She frowned. "Why, I don't think so. My family are pretty much all in Ohio or Pennsylvania, except Uncle Herbert . . ."

"Just a thought." He wagged his head. "Listen to my consummate rudeness. I've been mixing with the locals too long; my manners are suffering." He stepped back and bowed curtly. "My name is John Harrison Carter. I'm associated with Yale University and the Peabody Museum, working on a paleontological survey of this region. I'm very pleased to meet you, Miss Morrison."

"Yale. How splendid. I'm afraid my higher education is limited to Bowling Green's Normal School in Ohio. I'm a teacher most recently from Santa Fe, traveling west. I became lost and that stranger gave me a ride. I fear he's done you a disservice, dumping me upon you so precipitously."

"A disservice? Never. An honor." Phoebus waved a hand toward the tents. "Would you join me? Have you had breakfast?"

"A bit. I don't want to disrupt, really. I had no idea I was even coming here until we arrived."

"Perhaps some tea and biscuits."

"That would be very nice. Thank you."

"How propitious I decided to catch up on my records this morning. Normally I would have gone out into the field hours ago. Welcome to my simple camp."

Simple? The three tents were pitched perhaps twenty feet apart, facing the center of camp and forming three points of a triangle. A crude but sturdy wooden table marked the middle of the triangle. The chairs were clever wood-and-canvas folding stools. A blackened fire pit marked the cooktent, but the curl of smoke she had seen drifted from a stovepipe sticking out the back. Between two of the tents stood a table covered with papers and gray-white rocks. A mirror hung from the center pole of the right-hand tent, just above a washstand with towels, ewer, and basin. Phoebus might be camping, but here were all the comforts of home. Simple, indeed!

A dumpy little Spanish lady appeared in the flap of the cooktent.

"Tea and biscuits, Felicidad."

"Sí, señor." The lady disappeared inside.

Phoebus scooped up a folding stool and plunked it down by Naomi. She sat. It was wonderful to sit upon something which did not jog or sway or change directions unexpectedly. Most particularly being surrounded by the accoutrements of civilization delighted her, however rustic they might be.

Mr. Carter sat down a respectable distance away. "Were you being apologetic about your training? You should be proud of a normal school education. That's quite an accomplishment for a woman. We both know that education is the key to eliminating crime and poverty. Indeed, teaching is the noblest of all professions."

"I'm inclined to agree with that last statement. You mentioned a survey of some sort. You are a cartographer? Are you drawing the maps?"

"Filling them in." His eyes lighted like those of a small boy with a brand-new sled. "Let me show you." He hopped up and extended his hand. She rose and permitted him to lead her to the small table between the tents. His hand was warm and strong, the sort of hand needed to control the sun chariot's raging steeds. The papers she had first noticed were maps, an impressive array of maps which spread all over the table and curled down off its edges.

He tapped the corner of the topmost sheet. "Here's the area we intend to explore this afternoon. This line is that ridge right behind us; here's the wash, you see. This area right here interests me most. Triassic shale. And this map here . . ." He yanked another from under a rock. "This map has been filled in. You see, I penciled in the exact sites of promising layers and pockets."

"Layers which promise what, exactly?"

"Dinosaurs, Miss Morrison."

She frowned. "There are dinosaur footprints in, I believe, Connecticut. I remember the beasts as being described as monstrous lizards, long dead. They're out here, too?"

"Many more than back east, apparently. Vast deposits. Whole graveyards full. Have you ever heard of Dr. Othniel Marsh?"

"No."

"He chairs paleontology at Yale. Presently he's engaged in what you might call a contest of skills with a man named Edward Cope, and I daresay Cope is playing dirty, to use the vernacular. Their mutual object is to discover and name North America's extinct dinosaurs. Yale/Peabody sends out survey parties such as mine to scout likely areas for fossil-bearing strata. We send word of the choicest spots to New Haven and Dr. Marsh then dispatches work crews who perform the actual excavations."

"You are the vanguard, then, upon whom depends the success of Dr. Marsh's efforts."

"You flatter me. But that's pretty much it. You see . . . Ah! Here's the tea." He conducted her to the larger table and set a stool for her, seating her as though they were in the dining room of the Grand Hotel. She basked in the moment. Felicidad poured from a gracefully fluted pot.

"I compliment your lovely china . . . You mentioned a contest, Mr. Carter. A race?" The tea looked and smelled especially appealing in the wake of Linc's corrosive coffee.

"A race to find and name new kinds, with great prestige to the winner."

"May I ask who leads?"

"Dr. Marsh, by a comfortable margin, but the race isn't over."

"Then it's all rather like a treasure hunt."

"To me it's that precisely—a treasure hunt." He hesitated and his gray eyes smiled. "Dinosaurs are priceless. If they're not found they'll never be known, and if their remains are destroyed by careless handling or such, they can never be replaced.''

"You are enjoying the thrill of the chase, aren't you? It's written all over you." She was hungrier than she thought; her biscuits were disappearing quickly. "Does Dr. Marsh provide all this, or are you an independently wealthy connoisseur?"

"Dr. Marsh provides munificently. The black box over there." He pointed.

She turned to look. "It appears rather like a camera, but it's so small. I thought cameras were bigger."

"The newest thing, out just last year. Not only is this model easily portable, it employs a gelatin-emulsion film which produces good results in one twenty-fifth second. And in this country, with the bright sun and stark lines, my results are particularly sharp. Dry plate, of course. The wet plate collodion system went out years ago."

"Of course. Very impressive, all of this." She fished about for more questions simply to enjoy his boyish eagerness. Boyish. She thought about Linc Rawlins' artless ways. It was not at all the same sort of boyishness this man displayed. Mr. Carter's was pure and untrammeled enthusiasm. He was so very proud of his tools, his work, his position, his profession. Yet for all his bounding about and his enthusiasm, his impressive dignity was in no way diminished.

He stopped in the middle of a sentence about film developing. "Why am I talking on and on? The proper topic is you, not photographic chemistry. You say you're traveling west. How far?"

"To the ocean. But frankly I prefer your topics of conversation. I'm feeling increasingly vague about my own. Will you be going to Flagstaff soon?"

"I'm afraid not. I intend to work north, cross the river at

Lee's Ferry, and then survey my way across the Kaibab, so to speak. When I pick up the Colorado River again southbound, below the canyon, I'll be more or less out of mesozoic sediments and therefore out of dinosaur country. I'll float the river down to Needles and take the train from there home to New Haven.''

"Then your survey is nearly complete.''

"This one. Three months more, or four. I may end up on another, but I think all my peregrinations are about at an end. I'd like to settle into a nice quiet professorship at Yale and leave this rough-and-tumble travel to others. Let someone else freeze and roast and get snowed upon. I've done my penance.''

A professorship at Yale. Her mind and her dreams savored the phrase. She smiled. "Your wife will be so happy to see you home at last.''

He smiled, too. "I've never married. I'm afraid chasing old bones and properly attending a bride just don't mix.'' The smile faded. "Interesting. Here I assumed no educated woman—that is, no woman of refinement—would so much as lay eyes on this remote wilderness. Here you are to disprove me. You're obviously very finely bred, and yet you get along . . . I feel my mouth assuming the shape of my foot. How shall I say this? You fit in without letting the rough existence coarsen your behavior in any way whatever. Did I get through that without offending you?''

She felt radiant. "Take offense at such a lovely compliment? Really! This sounds false. Phony. But I insist to you it is not. That's exactly what I've been thinking about you just now. I was beginning to despair of enjoying refined company. The primary reason I'm traveling to San Francisco is to find some. I hunger for art, music, drama, a man in a proper suit and tie . . .''

"Hunger. Well put. You'll starve out here for that sort of

thing." He folded his napkin. "All this leaves the question of your immediate future hanging. I can't very well abandon what I'm doing here. The unseasonal weather has put me way behind schedule."

"Snow this late in the spring."

"Ridiculous. We should be experiencing summer weather by now. Instead we get summer snow. I understand weather is unseasonal all over the country this year. All the same, I can't just stop here. I can, however, release one of my guides to conduct you safely to Flagstaff. And there's another option. You're welcome to accompany our party here north to Lee's Ferry. From there, you'll surely find other parties traveling west. We should reach the river inside of three weeks."

Their eyes met and held. It was difficult to speak. He seemed to be groping for words also. She spoke first. "I trust your intentions completely, Mr. Carter. Please don't misconstrue my remarks. But there is the matter of appearances. An unwed woman traveling with an unwed man, even under these extenuating circumstances, invites stern frowns and arched eyebrows. My reputation is uncolored and I want to keep it that way. Even more importantly, a man in your position, with your expectations, should also be able to present a faultless reputation. I would love to accompany your party north, but, ah . . ." She spread her hands helplessly.

"An excellent point." He studied her seriously a moment, then broke into a dazzling smile. "A day or so, though, can't possibly strain the appearance of innocence. As you say, the circumstances are extenuating. We needn't work out the solution instantly. I'm sure we'll come up with something amenable." The beautiful, even teeth befitted a Greek god. "And I'll state for the record right here and now that I'll keep a proper distance."

"I had no doubts, sir."

He rose and bowed slightly. "If you'll excuse me, then, I must be going. I'll try to be back early this afternoon. Felicidad will arrange guest quarters for you with her in the cooktent. Please consider her in your service as well as in mine."

Naomi stammered appreciatively, and he responded in kind. With seeming reluctance he moved away, spoke briefly at the cooktent flap and jogged off down the hill to the waiting horses. Felicidad trundled out and began clearing the table.

Naomi sat and let the appearance of him linger in her mind awhile. She stood up and stretched, then walked over to the mirror. She dreaded looking at it. Linc impishly called her *nizhoni*—pretty. Under normal circumstances she was. It's certainly not prideful to recognize one's physical attributes, but circumstances were not normal. She peeked in the glass.

As she feared, the looks of her hair confirmed the fact that her hairbrushes must be in Flagstaff. Her eyes had developed unbecoming little circles. Her cheeks were darker than she'd ever seen them, and her normally creamy complexion was sun-baked past admiration. To top it all her nose was peeling. She sighed. Here she was, coming face to face with Phoebus in the flesh, and her face was ghastly.

Phoebus. Apollo. There had to be something drastically wrong with the man. Nobody could be that perfect. She frowned at herself in the mirror. He claimed, essentially, that education was the salvation of the world. A Christian would insist that Jesus Christ is the ultimate answer to social unrest, to crime or to any other problem. Was John Carter one of those collegiate agnostics—or worse, an atheist—who discounted the Lord? She knew perfectly well Scripture warned against being unevenly yoked with such an unbeliever.

The frown fled and she laughed out loud. What vain imaginings! She had known the man less than an hour, and already she was thinking about the yoke of marriage. How ridiculous. How dreadfully silly.

His religious views were topics to explore in the comfort of evening tea and gathering darkness. She filled her lungs with this clear and twinkling desert air. Her spirits, dampened both figuratively and literally by the night before, soared again. Rain and darkness were past. Gone was the season's last snow. Linc said so.

Only brightness lay ahead now.

Sunshine.

Phoebus.

CHAPTER 5

IT WAS A TINY HOLE in the earth—scarcely bigger than the capital O in a book text. Yet how many thousands of minuscule feet scrambled in and out it! Each tiny black ant entering the hole carried a neatly clipped bit of green leaf. Each emergent ant departed, unburdened. Five streams of ants radiated from the hole; in addition, stray individuals wandered about to the tunes of different drummers. Each ant invariably greeted any other passing ant, a constant howde-do of pauses and feeler-tappings.

Naomi perched on her folding stool, her elbows on her knees, and watched the scurrying insects wave their incessant hellos. She imagined stopping to greet every pedestrian one chanced to meet in, say, downtown Toledo. Preposterous.

She sat up straight and stretched her back. Her eyes drifted to the horizon, a flat line of ridges to the east which John called Ward Terrace. She gasped and shaded her eyes. A rider was watching the camp. She could see no detail at this distance, but she could tell the rider was bareheaded.

Out west, it was axiomatic that white men wore the hats. Some years ago in southern Arizona, a rancher named Pete Kitchen, beleaguered by marauding Apaches, told his cowboys to shoot anyone not wearing a hat. Now where had she read that? *Leslie's Illustrated Weekly?*

A little chill tittered down her spine. She didn't like Joe Dasanie, the taller of John's scouts, and she liked the short Neeskah even less. Unsmiling and withdrawn, they hung constantly like vultures on the periphery of the camp. John seemed to trust them. After all he had hired them. So they must be reliable or they wouldn't be here. Surely he had insisted upon excellent references. But their sullen ways made her uneasy. Still, that rider on the ridge was their kind. Were they friends or strangers? Was that watcher Joe Dasanie?

The waning sun splashed fire across the scarp. She remembered fondly the nearness and leafy shade of Ohio farm country. Back there, sunset meant simply gathering darkness and perhaps some lovely color in the western sky. Out here, come sundown, land and sky together went out in a blaze of glory. The scarp turned from red to glowing purple. The rider disappeared.

She pulled her cape close around. Her hands trembled a little. She must be unusually sensitive to cold because of last night's chill. The sun-splashed vastness of the desert around their little knob grayed.

Two miles to the east, a dust cloud materialized. That should be John returning for the evening. How quickly wet ground dried to dust. Or was it John? She watched uneasily until she could clearly discern his blaze-faced sorrel. Joe Dasanie followed on his chunky and big-headed bay. He was leading a mule, heavily laden. And from the northeast, here came Neeskah on his ragged little roan. None of the three came from the immediate vicinity of that watcher.

John left Dasanie in his dust and rode the last half-mile at a rollicking canter. Naomi walked out to greet him as he dismounted. He dropped his horse's reins and tipped his hat.

"Splendid day! Found some late Triassic with identifiable cycadeoid fronds."

"I assume that's promising."

"Absolutely!" Seemingly without thinking, he took her hand in his and started back to the tents. She did not pull away. "Right time period, and the fronds confirm a terrestrial flora. Had I found marine forms, you see, there would be no dinosaurs—dinosaurs being essentially terrestrials."

"Wouldn't just any fossil be important? I mean—not only dinosaurs, but any ancient thing?"

"Oh, I suppose. Dr. Cope is engaged in naming anything he can lay hands on, living or dead. But Dr. Marsh specializes. Therefore, so do I."

"Mmm." Naomi felt warmer. This man's enthusiasm rubbed off; his vigor inspired. She wanted to leap and bounce.

The sun was nearly gone now. The ridge plunged from purple to dark, stolid gray.

"I saw an Indian this evening, spying on us from that ridge over there." She pointed. "I don't think it was either of your two."

"Spying? Or simply curious?"

"Watching."

He released her hand and dragged two folding stools into close proximity. "I wouldn't worry about it. There are savages all over the area—Navajos mostly, some Hopi now and then. I have no business with them, nor am I looking for anything they could possibly want." He smiled. The hazel eyes danced. "This is the first time I have ever returned to a pretty face come evening. There's much to be said for domestic bliss."

39

She giggled and plopped down on a stool. Maybe the peeling on her nose was not so bad after all. "No mother? No sister? No cute little lap terrier?"

He responded impishly, almost flirtatiously, but she didn't hear. A movement beyond him caught her eye. Joe Dasanie was spying, and there was no other word for it. He watched them furtively from beyond the far tent. His eyes flicked past John to meet hers. Then he slipped quickly away behind the canvas.

"Mr. Carter? How thoroughly do you screen your guides?"

"Not at all. What's to screen? They know the area, they were available, they liked the pay. They handle animals well, though a bit roughly, and they're trainable in terms of learning how to pick out bedding layers. They are a little slack in the traces when it comes to moving out in the morning and getting a good jump on the day. Tend to wander off at night. All in all, they're adequate for my needs."

"You've no reservations about them at all?"

"No, no, no, my dear. You have it backwards. We don't have reservations; Indians have reservations. Vast ones."

Her cheeks and ears turned warm in her effort to suppress laughter. After all, loud laughter was not lady-like, and she so wanted him to consider her a well-bred lady. She managed to compress it all into a demure and hand-held giggle. She took a deep breath. "You've been associating with pick-up help for years, and you trust them. Therefore, my suspicions are mine alone, and unfounded. Shame on me for questioning your judgment."

"Shame? Hardly. I'm flattered. It shows your concern." He turned serious. "And that pleases me, that you should be concerned." He stood up suddenly and stuck his head inside the cooktent flap. "Felicidad? When is dinner served?"

"Half-hour maybe. I din' know when you come."

"Very well." He stood straight and turned to Naomi. "Would you be interested in a pre-dinner stroll, Miss Morrison?"

She stood up and laid her hand upon his extended arm. "Delighted, Mr. Carter."

They ambled downhill toward the green and winding wash. Perhaps she would find some of the season's first little annuals blooming in the sand.

Naomi drew a happy sigh. "All these rocks look alike to me. How would I know if I were looking at a dinosaur?"

"The rock has to be sedimentary. Layered. Then, irregularities are your first clue. Lumps, dents, lines and marks, inclusions of a different color or texture. Next, you examine more closely by breaking up likely rocks, chipping to fresh material—I don't know how to answer precisely. It comes with practice. The tyro spots only the most obvious—skulls grinning up at him, you might say. The experienced paleontologist sees fossils where no one else does."

"In essence, you've been out looking for lumps in rocks all day."

His laugh was rumbling and genuine. He probably sang baritone. "Better than digging ditches. I suppose I must admit that even the experienced hunter must be graced with incredible luck, but we professionals don't like to ascribe our success to luck. Tarnishes the shining image."

She had three different comments to make on shining images, not excluding references to Phoebus and his chariot, but she held her tongue. A lady is never forward.

He laid a warm hand on top of hers. "And what did you do this afternoon?"

"Watched an ant's nest for the better part of an hour. Intriguing, though I almost fell asleep. I read parts of your geology book; well, to be honest, I looked at drawings and

41

captions. Also that book on paleobotany by Williamson. I stand in awe of your knowledge and your work.''

He smiled modestly. Charming. ''The Williamson text was especially helpful up around the Hopi mesas. Coal seams there, and Williamson dwells primarily with the paleobotany of coal formations, as you now know. Moreover, he . . .''

John continued, his enthusiasm unabated, but Naomi missed most of his lecture. Her attention had been snatched by Neeskah, who stood down by a pothole in the wash. Ostensibly the guide was watering the horses and mules. The five animals jostled each other, dipping their heads low to reach water level in the tiny *tinaja*. But Neeskah was watching John and Naomi on their stroll. He did not face them squarely and watch like an honest man. He followed them stealthily with his eyes, feigning disinterest. A chill crept down her back.

John was winding up his discourse with a flourish. ''. . . these hills especially. You call my quest a treasure hunt. If these latest findings are what I hope them to be, I've discovered pure gold.''

He uttered those last words loudly. Neeskah stiffened slightly at the mention of gold. And now he started up the hill with his animals in tow, watching closely and still pretending he was not.

John stopped. ''You've turned cold, Miss Morrison. What's wrong? What did I say?''

''Nothing. I'm sorry. I just . . .'' She watched Neeskah disappear beyond the tents. ''He was watching us again.''

''I understand that's Navajo custom, and he's half Navajo. Don't know about Apaches, his other half. Among Navajos, you never let on that you're watching someone else. You may live in the middle of a ten-mile basin, and, when a visitor comes to call, even if you have seen him

42

coming for five miles, you always pretend surprise when he shows up at your door. It's a strange little custom."

She shook her head. "All the same, I distrust your guides. I'm sorry, and I don't mean to cast doubts on your good judgment, but they make me nervous. I suggest we give personal safety a greater emphasis in our prayers tonight."

He took both her hands in his. "You really are frightened. Your fingers are cold. I'm sorry you feel this way. Believe me, if I could get along without them, I'd dismiss them both this minute just to make you feel better."

"You would?" She looked into his eyes. He would. She stared at his hands. "Thank you. That's very thoughtful." His hands were tough without being rough. He groveled in dirt constantly, yet his fingernails were clean. The strong hands tightened on hers.

She looked up into his weather-browned face. Phoebus.

"Miss Morrison. Uh . . . Naomi." He licked his lips. Whatever he had in mind fled his chambers before he could say it. Those radiant eyes scanned her nose, her chin, her cheeks. They peered earnestly into her own eyes. They dwelt thoughtfully upon her lips.

Did he really care enough about her that he would ease her mind with such drastic action (were he able, of course)? The thought delighted her and struck dread in her simultaneously. Such care suggests a far deeper relationship than she was prepared for. Moreover, in such a relationship, fraught with concern and self-sacrifice, it would be very, very easy to transgress the bounds of propriety. They must observe caution here, extreme caution. She parted her lips to tell him so, but only silence spoke.

Not content to study her from the more seemly distance of twelve or fifteen inches, his eyes moved in for a closer look, of necessity bringing his lips along. She realized this rather

43

belatedly, much too late to back away. His lips brushed across hers, but the gesture seemed proper enough so long as both of them maintained a civilized reserve. Now his lips were on hers fairly, pressing, working. The kiss would surely remain respectable so long as their hands remained intertwined.

His hands released hers and surrounded her, pushed against her back, drew her in close and tight. No matter—the kiss was harmless so long as they remained there. But now his lips were forcing her head aside to snuggle deep and firm against his broad shoulder. One hand gripped the small of her back. The other massaged her shoulder ("Where the wings will grow," her mother always said). She was squeezed into him, encompassed by his strength, enveloped in his ardent bulk. She felt so warm.

Warmth. A few short hours ago, freezing rain and snow had robbed all her warmth until she was past caring. Today she was smothered in warmth of the most marvelous sort; and oh, she cared! But she must put a stop to this before things got out of hand. At the same time, she dare not resist or speak for fear it would stop.

"Deener's ready!" Felicidad's excessively cheery voice pealed down the hillside.

John disconnected reluctantly. He scooped her hands back into his. "Rest assured this won't happen again." The hazel eyes laughed. "Unless, of course, I'm very, very lucky."

She felt the heat rise in her cheeks and neck. She must be glowing red as a desert sunset. What should she say? She solved that dilemma by saying nothing. They strolled up the hill hand-in-hand, in silence.

Just before they stepped in among the tents, Naomi glanced off toward the ridge.

The watcher was there.

44

CHAPTER 6

ONLY ONCE BEFORE in this year of 1889 had Naomi Morrison eaten in a fine restaurant. It was a charming little place in Santa Fe, down the street from the Hotel Valencia. And because it served in direct competition with the hotel dining room, its prices were within the means of a struggling spinster teacher.

Tonight she felt as if she were again seated in that elegant restaurant. Felicidad was not exactly a maitre d', nor was the starry sky a pressed tin ceiling, nor did the canvas tents approximate tapestries and draperies. The oil lamp sputtered, a poor substitute for a chandelier. The menu was beans, tortillas, and jackrabbit. The difference? Phoebus.

John Carter treated her elegantly, maintained a witty and varied conversation, displayed impeccable manners. Naomi's heart sang for the pure joy of lounging in the full embrace of civilization.

They discussed ways of choosing a fine restaurant. They expressed mutual relief that the profligate lifestyles of such as Byron and Shelley were being eclipsed by the new wave of poets with a stronger morality—the Brownings, Tennyson, Longfellow. In a few minutes' brief discussion, they solved the knotty problem of the British presence in China. However pleasant and stimulating the conversation, though, she could only apply part of her faculties to it. The remainder, the back of her mind, dwelt upon that kiss.

It was certainly not her first kiss. There was Horace back in normal school, whom she dropped when he tried to go exploring as they rode in a hansom cab. There was Morris, a fellow schoolteacher at Toledo's Park Street Academy. Only a persistent twitch of his right eye marred his handsome appearance. She ended their relationship when he tried to convince her that the twitch would be cured permanently if only she would spend the night at his apartment. A charming young man whom she had met en route to Santa Fe, as it turned out, was still securely married to the harridan he had just abandoned. And there was the long string of hopefuls who tag along after any unattached woman in a land of many men and few ladies. Most of them found their first kiss to be their last, if they got even that far.

But John was another matter altogether. Was she wantonly pursuing the man simply because he had a foot in the door of one of the nation's most prestigious universities? The Yale connection certainly didn't hurt. But as she mulled over the matter, she convinced herself that the magnet was the man himself. He was certainly no monk; his kiss said plainly that he knew his way with a woman. After all, he was probably in his thirties, if only barely so. One must be realistic about men's appetites, about sowing wild oats and all that sort of rubbish. He possessed all the characteristics she attributed to the man of her dreams. And yet there was more to him than all that. He was attractive beyond his physical particulars, his education, his promising future.

Phoebus.

Linc Rawlins popped into her mind unbidden. Now why should she think of him? In fact, the more she compared the two men, the more surprised she was that she should think of him at all. Everything John *was* Linc was *not*—past, present and future.

"I said, 'Your tea is getting cold.' " His voice snapped her back to the moment.

"I apologize. My mind was wandering."

"Through private gardens, or may I join your thoughts?"

"You're already in them." Her ears were getting warm again.

"Mmm. You mean, earlier this evening?"

"Only in part," she lied.

He sat back smiling. "Then I won't say another word. Go back to your mental meandering and I'll do the same, content that I'm in your thoughts just as you're in mine."

"I wish life were that simple."

"Isn't it?"

"Don't act so innocent, John Carter. You're a dangerous man. Your sophistication isn't just the external polish of manners and education. You're accustomed to, shall we say, relating comfortably to a woman in whatever capacity you care to extend that relationship. In other words, I'm no match for a man who knows both what he wants and how to obtain it. As regards men, I am much too ignorant for my own good. I'm leery of you now."

He sobered. "I told you at the outset that I'm trustworthy, and you said you did, in fact, trust me. Nothing has changed. A harlot is one thing, but a proper lady is quite another altogether. I'd never take unfair advantage of you. Never."

"Nor would I let you, under normal circumstances. This evening wasn't normal. When we were, ah, wrapped up in the enthusiasm of the moment, I don't believe either of us was trustworthy. It's all well and good to discuss a relationship objectively as we sit across the table from each other here. But when two people are close—I mean, very close—" she shook her head. "It's no longer simply a matter of appearances. Appearances may be how the world judges us, but God judges us otherwise. You're a powerful temptation, and I think I should leave immediately."

Her statement startled her. She had not been thinking that at all. And yet as she heard herself speaking the words, she knew it was true.

Was he bemused by her prudishness or irritated by her lack of trust? The corner of his mouth turned up in a fascinating way. He plunked both elbows on the table—not very mannerly, but out here, so what?—and propped his chin in the cup of one hand. He studied her several moments. "You know, you're even more beautiful when you're being virtuous."

She gasped. "And just when do you think I'm *not* being virtuous?!"

His eyes were laughing. He was teasing and she had walked right into it. She sat back, chagrined.

"You know," he said, still looking into her eyes, "when that half-breed dumped you here, the first thing I . . ."

"Half-breed? Why do you think he's of mixed ancestry?"

"No pure Navajo has a build that tall or hair that short. Trust me. He's a breed."

"You happen to be correct. I just wondered why you assumed that?"

"Never mind him. He's in the past and gone. As I was saying, when he dumped you here, I was irritated at the intrusion. The last thing I needed was some little waif hanging around my neck like an albatross. Here it is, less than eight hours later, and I'm so very glad you came. I'm sorry I frightened you, but I want you to stay. Your terms.

Your conditions. But don't go yet. I enjoy your company from across the table, or six feet away, or however far you wish. I even like the way your nose is shedding."

She smiled in spite of herself. "May I speak frankly?"

"Of course."

"You may mean what you say. You may even abide by the same Christian principles I adhere to. But if you're a lecher with deep dark plans, the two things you would hasten to assure me would be: one, that you're trustworthy; two, that I shouldn't leave. I simply don't know you well enough. Do you see my point?"

He nodded. "Clearly. You can't hang onto your moral integrity by glibly believing every Tom, Dick and Harry who passes. Or John, as the case may be. I'm afraid I have to concur. You might, though, give some of us the benefit of the doubt."

"And I'm sure some of you deserve it. But I don't know which ones. I think perhaps I should leave for Flagstaff tomorrow morning, first thing."

"And hop a train?"

"No money. I have to earn the train fare first. I'm done with stagecoaches. It has to be the railroad all the way."

He joined his fingertips; they diddled on each other at the apex of the triangle. "You don't want to leave Flag much before May at the earliest. The Sierra passes are snowed in, hard to travel. In fact, Flag gets snowed in regularly. Will you wait for me there in Flagstaff?"

She cocked her head. "Until you finish this survey?"

"No promises, understand. I'm not suggesting marriage or betrothal or anything of the sort. But I'd like to get to know you better—under less tempting circumstances, if you insist. May fifteenth. No, the twenty-first. If I can't be in Flag by May twenty-first the long way, I'll cut the survey short and come straight in."

49

"You'd short-change your survey just for me?"

He shrugged. "From Lee's Ferry, or maybe Red Mesa, on over, most formations are limestone, I understand. Marine sediments; no good for dinosaurs anyway. Besides, I'm pretty certain I've found enough right in here to keep Dr. Marsh's crews busy. I can cut back some with a clear conscience."

"Well, uh . . ." She smiled. This was Phoebus speaking to her! "If I can't find a paying position in Flagstaff, uh, I'll be in Prescott. Surely between the two major towns I can find something." The smile fled. "Now how do I get to Flagstaff?"

He grimaced. "I realize you don't like my guides, but I don't see any alternative. The weather's put me too far behind here—especially if I hope to be back in Flag by the twenty-first. Joe Dasanie is probably the quicker of the two. I'll send him along with orders to see you safely to town and then return immediately."

"I don't really think I . . ."

"You'll be safer with him than you would with a white guide. If anything happened to a white woman for whom he's responsible, he'd hang before the sun sets and he knows it. He knows I know where you're going and how long it will take to get there and back. And, he knows I'll be checking up on you. He has no choice but to deliver you swiftly and safely wherever you want to go."

The thought of entrusting herself to that rascal, even for a few days, bothered her. But John's points made sense. "Well, if you're certain you can do without him."

"Then it's settled. Felicidad, more tea, please."

They talked for hours that night. John was unflaggingly loquacious and cheery, and it made her feel just as bubbly. They lingered over breakfast the next day and dawdled over good-bys. Many times Naomi came close to deciding to stay. But each time she felt a bit overwhelmed by his charm, she remembered also the temptation he presented. She was near tears when they kissed in parting and she climbed into the saddle of Joe Dasanie's horse. Already the morning was half spent. She twisted in the saddle to wave one final good-by before they followed the curving wash out of sight.

By noon Naomi was perilously close to telling Joe Dasanie to turn around. She wanted to follow John's party the full distance of the survey loop. She wanted to float down the Colorado River. She loved the scenery in these deserts; to travel through them in such comfort as John's camp afforded made the scenery even more inviting.

And of course there was the man himself. Phoebus. She imagined floating down the river with him, strolling in the moonlight, watching scarps glow in the sunset. . . . She hardened her resolve to hurry on to town. There was the whole reason she must leave. Her virtue would never survive the trip. Not with that man.

Joe Dasanie, rid' .g John's extra pack mule, stopped for lunch in a quiet little wash. Her head might have been in the clouds, but her backside was complaining bitterly. She remembered the cushiony seat Linc Rawlins' bedroll provided, and transferred her own bedroll from the back of her saddle to the seat. The padding helped, but not much. By nightfall the insides of her legs ached dreadfully.

That discomfort was nothing, however, compared to the stiffness and pain the next morning. How did people manage to ride horses for days—nay, even years—on end? "On end." A good pun, that, but not one for polite company.

On the other hand, Joe Dasanie was hardly polite company. He was by turns haughty or secretive, but never polite.

By noon the sky, once blue, turned gray. Without the sun Naomi quickly got cold. No doubt about it—that awful night when she had chilled so thoroughly had ruined her temperature balance, at least temporarily.

The overcast thickened. Soon she could barely discern which part of the sky contained the sun. It should be directly before them, but instead the sun hung forlornly over their right shoulders. She twisted in the saddle, a painful process, to make certain and reined in her horse. It sighed, stretched its neck, and shook its mane.

"Joe, that's south. That way. We're headed east."

"Gonna rain."

"It feels like it. But I don't . . ."

"Hole up in ledges over there."

"But I don't want to ride an inch further than necessary. We must press on, in rain if need be. Every yard we go east we must ride west again. You'll take me directly to Flagstaff with no deviations, rain or no."

He smirked. Suddenly he snatched the reins from her hand. Her horse's back end swung aside as he jerked the looped reins up over its head. Naomi gripped the saddle horn to keep from tumbling. He slammed his heels into his mule's ribs and dragged Naomi's horse along behind. They were headed directly east.

"Stop! We're going the other way, do you hear? John Carter will have your head if you don't cooperate. Stop!"

Her horse shifted from a clumsy trot to a rocking-horse lope which threatened to unseat her with every stride. The muscles of her inner thighs screamed in protest. She could feel an open sore where a seam of her pantaloons rubbed between the saddle and her fanny. She should jump off, but she was much too frightened to try. She should lean forward and try to wrest back control of her horse, but she'd fall for sure. She should shriek loudly enough to arouse banshees in the Irish quarter of San Francisco, but there was no one to hear. She was alone in an alien wilderness.

52

All the little chills and misgivings she had ever entertained toward Dasanie and Neeskah congealed into a solid lump of fear. It lodged at the base of her throat to steal both her breath and her reason.

The cliff which marked a mesa rim once lay in the distance to their left. Now they were hard upon it and driving straight at it full bore. The horses clawed their way up a steep gravel slope. Ahead, a solid wall of rock barred the way. Where could he be going?

Suddenly Dasanie turned his mule broadside, directly in front of her. Her horse squealed and sat back on its haunches to avoid colliding. With a horrified little yelp, she slid across the sweaty neck and landed in the dirt. Hooves clattered and churned all around her.

Joe Dasanie was laughing.

She stood up and brushed dirt from her skirts and arms. "Joe Dasanie, that was deliberate! You'll pay dearly for this."

"No." His voice took on an ominous edge that made her cringe. "No, I won't pay. Your John Carter, he's gonna pay. He likes you. So first I take you in payment. Then when he finds his gold, we collect the rest of our pay from him."

"Gold? You're much mistaken. He's not after gold. He's . . ."

"Bah!" Dasanie spat the word so violently she stopped in mid-breath. "He's foolish, but not so foolish he spends all this time and money looking for bones. No bones. That's a lie. Every other Anglo we ever see wants gold, so don't lie to me. That's what he's looking for. We heard him."

"We. So you and Neeskah are together in this. You're going to rob him! Do you realize what will happen to you two if you so much as think about it?"

"We get trouble only if you or him live to tell someone. Carter won' live, and you won' tell nobody."

She stammered, her reeling mind temporarily disconnected from her speech. "No." She shook her head. "No, I don't think either of you is that stupid. Besides, John did nothing to invite your wrath."

"Fancy words. No wonder you two like each other. You come to me now. I'm gonna spoil you; Carter or nobody gonna want you."

"Why do you hate him so?" She must keep him talking.

"Don' matter."

"Of course it matters."

"He thinks we're dirt."

"That's hardly reason to . . ."

"Some Mex in a red shirt stole a fella's horse and money. That's all; didn't kill him or nothin'. They hung my brother because he was wearing a red shirt and he was handy. All look alike you know—Mexicans and Indians." His voice rose. "That kinda stuff all the time."

"But surely Neeskah doesn't want to . . ."

"Neeskah got his own reasons—same kinda reasons."

"But John certainly isn't responsible."

"Mexicans and Indians, they don' all look alike. Whites, *they* all look alike. Lotsa paying back to do. Carter, you, others. Lotsa others. You come to me."

Escape was impossible. She knew that, but she wheeled to run anyway. He caught her, gripped her arm, yanked her to a halt within three strides.

She was doomed. She would be the first of their victims, or perhaps just one more in a nameless procession. She would be ravished and murdered, to disappear forever from the face of the earth in an unmarked grave at the base of some nameless mesa.

And John Carter, who was so marvelous and had so much to offer the world, would be their next victim.

CHAPTER 7

EVERYBODY SAYS THAT when death is imminent, your whole life flashes before your eyes. Well, everyone was wrong. In those long terrifying moments, Naomi could think of nothing but escape. She twisted and tugged but the struggle was an empty gesture, something a victim ought to do when disaster is certain.

He yanked at her cape. The wool collar burned across her neck, the button popped, and the cape was gone. He clawed at the front of her dress to no avail. It was too sturdy to tear.

She prayed earnestly even as she struggled. She cried out aloud to God, but her faith wavered. Even if He heard— surely He heard!—what could He do? She nearly broke free for a moment, but "nearly" falls woefully short of "definitely" when your honor and your very life are on the line. She was helpless, and that enraged her. Yet even the rage did not give her strength to resist effectively.

Struggle wasn't helping. Suddenly she stopped struggling and lunged against Dasanie. The reversal threw him off balance for a second; in that second she spun in place, a full circle that tore his grip loose. She started running. She could not even see where she was going.

From nowhere a hand snatched her arm and yanked her aside. She slammed into the crumbling cliff face. Neeskah was here, too! John must be dead already and she was ruined!

But the owner of that hand was a foot taller than Neeskah and half as wide. Abraham Lincoln Rawlins loomed between her and her attacker.

Dasanie sneered something derisive in Navajo. He repeated it. His hand flashed to his side. Before Naomi could warn Linc about Dasanie's eight-inch hunting knife, it was balanced on his fingertips. He dropped to a menacing crouch.

Naomi gulped. Linc owned a weapon equally long, and he was equally deft at readying it. Its tip wavered and danced practically in front of her nose. Linc let go her arm and wiggled his fingers. She placed her hand in his. Brandishing his knife, he circled wide, out away from the cliff toward the horses. Dasanie spoke again, pivoting in place. But for those hideous blades, the confrontation would have seemed a colossal staring match.

Linc shoved her toward the horses without taking his eyes off Dasanie. "Get me his horse." Linc leaped forward and snatched her abandoned cape off the ground. With a wide sweep and a snap he wound it loosely over his left arm. She was now protected by a gladiator replete with eight-inch sword and woolen shield.

The mule had disappeared, but Dasanie's horse still stood there, its reins dragging the ground. It backed up several steps before she finally managed to catch it. She grabbed the looped reins and hung on.

Dasanie spoke again in Navajo, then switched to English. "You picked the wrong fight, breed."

"Not this time. Naomi, give him his horse. Let him go."

56

"No! He intends to rob John, perhaps even kill him!"

"I said give him his horse!"

"Please don't let him go!" Her shouting and the tension made the horse jittery. It waltzed, heavy-footed, in a circle around her.

"Yeah," Dasanie grinned, evil as Satan himself. " 'Don' let him go.' Come get me, breed. They treat you so pretty you wanna die for 'm, huh? She worth dying for, eh?"

"Nobody's gonna die." Linc extended his left hand toward Naomi, reaching for the horse's reins.

Dasanie lunged forward. Naomi heard herself scream. Lightning-fast, Linc swung the cape at Dasanie. It tipped the Indian aside, spoiling his aim. He leaped back. Her cape dangled in two separate tatters from Linc's arm.

Dasanie's face turned cold. "I watch your blood run out, breed. Then I stick your lady friend. You should never 'a tangled with me. You should never 'a put yourself on their side."

Linc sidestepped quickly, putting himself between Naomi and Dasanie. "Climb aboard and ride west, Naomi. Keep the cliff behind you."

"But what about you? He's . . ."

"Go!"

Naomi turned her attentions to the horse. She tried to throw the loop of reins up over the horse's busy ears. The nag tossed its obstinate head high and backed away from her. Its huge feet splacked in the dirt near her toes. She managed to loop the reins over one ear, but not the other. Behind her, she heard shuffling and grunting as the gladiators engaged. Frantically she tugged at the loop. The romal, that long braided quirt which formed the rein ends, tangled a moment in the mane hair by the horse's ear. It broke free and strapped her across the cheek hard enough to close one eye.

She was crying now. She tossed the loop again. It cleared the wagging ears. With one hand on the near rein, she tried to get her foot in the stirrup. It was too high, and the horse moved constantly. She jumped up and down on one foot, struggling.

The knife hilts clacked together. Again and again the hilts clacked, and the two men locked together nose-to-nose. Dasanie staggered backward and slashed out. His blade swooshed by much too close to Linc's throat. The horse nearly broke free of her grip. Thus reminded, she tried again to mount the horse.

But now the fight had come to her. Both men were lurching toward her, clutching each other, stabbing, gasping for breath. She dragged the horse's head aside to pull it out of their way. Linc slammed back against her and crushed her against the horse's shoulder. Dasanie's knife slashed wildly past her cheek.

The Indian grunted. Linc pushed away and the two men crashed together again like cymbals. Dasanie fell back, lost his footing and tumbled. He looked surprised for a moment, scrabbled to his feet, and ran off. He hunched his whole upper half together into a tight little knot.

Linc stumbled after Dasanie but gave up the pursuit almost immediately. Winded, he hopped onto a head-high boulder. He watched from a distance with his shoulders heaving, sucking in air. His knife blade was bloody.

Naomi dragged the horse over toward him. She watched his shoulders droop a little as the tension eased. A minute later he jumped down beside her and took the reins out of her trembling hands.

He mumbled something apologetic and returned her slashed cape.

What could she say? A mere "thank you" seemed so pitifully trite and shallow. She fingered the ragged slash in

58

her garment, grateful that Linc had been spared. She followed him silently across the slope, where, in the distance stood that lovely gray horse.

She walked up to its head and rubbed its nose. "Hello, Nizhoni, handsome old friend. I never thought I'd be so happy to see you again. I never thought I'd see you again at all." She turned to Linc. "How did you know? How did you come here?"

He flopped an arm across Nizhoni's withers and sagged wearily against the gray shoulder. "After I left you, I started back south toward my place. But then I thought, 'The weather's turned nice again. Why am I rushing off home?' I didn't have anything better to do for a couple days, so I turned around and went back up. Thought I might hang around awhile and make sure everything was going all right for you. I didn't know anything about that fancy eastern professor except what the Dineh told me in Leupp."

"That can't be too much. Dineh are Navajos, right?"

"It's what the Navajos call themselves, yeah."

"I doubt they understood or care in Leupp about what John is doing here in the territory. You must have heard some interesting things about him."

"If you guess they laugh about him, you're right."

Naomi stopped rubbing Nizhoni's chin. "That means you've been watching out for me. That rider east of John's camp on the ridge! That was you!"

"Mighta been." He looked the bay horse over. "Whose horse?"

"Joe Dasanie. The man you just drove off. Why have you been looking out for me like this?"

"Wish I knew. Climb up there." He flicked the bay's looped reins effortlessly over its ears.

Since he now held the horse she used both hands to steady its stirrup. She poked her toe into it and groped for the saddle horn. He planted the palm of one hand firmly on her backside and pushed. Gracelessly she sailed up and on. There he was again, being careless about where he touched a lady.

He swooped up onto Nizhoni in one fluid motion, making horsemanship look so effortless, so painless.

Her muscles and the open sore reminded her at once that the bedroll was not cushioning her posterior. She pointed off in the direction of the altercation. "My bedroll is somewhere there on the ground. I use it for—for padding." She glanced at him, almost guilty about asking still another favor. "May we go back for it, please?"

He clamped his legs around the big gray horse and he side-stepped, swinging around beside her.

"Stiff here?" And he had the temerity to point with a finger to precisely that part of his own anatomy.

"Approximately." Naomi felt her ears burn. She averted her eyes, embarrassed enough for both of them.

"Then a bulky pad is the last thing you want. It stretches your muscles even further and just makes it worse." He turned Nizhoni aside and started off.

"But aren't we going to go get my blanket anyway?" She had to drag her horse back; it seemed naturally to want to follow Nizhoni.

"Nope."

"Oh." She released the reins and kicked her horse's ribs. "Then we're hurrying right straight up to John to warn him, right?" Her pony fell in behind Nizhoni. "Dasanie and Neeskah—those are John's two guides, you know—they're in this together, both of them. They plan to rob John, perhaps even murder him, so he won't talk. But I still don't understand quite why. Nonetheless . . ."

"You asked him?"

"Of course. And he had no real reason other than a

generalized sort of bitterness, at least as far as I could see. Absolutely unjustified.''

"I doubt it.''

"You mean, you doubt he was justified.''

"I mean I can see how he might be bitter enough to tear apart your professor and you and the rest of the race.''

"Are you condoning robbery and murder and . . . and . . . unspeakable crimes?''

"Isn't an Indian in the territory doesn't have some reason to cut loose.''

"I can't believe you. Here you . . . oh, never mind. We're going back up to John's, right? Will we get there tonight? Can we ride all night, perhaps?''

"Nope.''

"Tomorrow then.''

"Not going there.''

"But we have to!''

"Look at the sky and feel the wind. It's gonna be a cold, wet couple days, and I don't want the trouble of thawing you out again. At least you were traveling in the right direction this time. My place is less than six hours away if we push it.''

"*Your* place! *Mister* Rawlins!'' She hauled her bay to a stop. It turned in a circle, impatient.

Linc pivoted Nizhoni and locked her eye-to-eye. "Yeah. I'm going back up to my place before this rain and maybe a little snow lets loose. I'm gonna build a roaring fire in the stove and get warm clear through for once. I'm gonna cook up a pot of beans and make some coffee that doesn't eat through the cup. I've been four solid weeks on the road and I'm gonna take it easy a couple days. Now if you care to tag along and get in out of the storm, you're welcome. If you think you best head north up to your precious John, that's your privilege. You're a big girl. You make the decision, whatever you want to do. I'm nobody's nursemaid and I'm done hovering over you like a hen with one chick.'' His voice was rising.

So was hers. ''But Dasanie's on his way right now to harm John! He said so!''

Linc's voice was a bit strident. ''Dasanie will be lucky to get through the night alive. I clipped his ribs good and half cut his arm off.''

''You don't have to yell at me, you know. It's not my fault he had mayhem on his mind. He asked for whatever he got.''

''Your precious body isn't so holy that it's worth a man's life to touch it. Had I known he was gonna take me on, I might never have waded into him. I wanted to scare him off you, that's all. I don't in the least like the idea that I might be responsible for a man's dying.''

''Then why don't you go back and apologize and take *him* home to your place? You realize if the fight had come out the other way, he would have harbored no compunctions whatever about ripping you apart.''

''Don't you think I know that? Why do you suppose we left that blanket roll behind? For the coyotes and ground squirrels?'' He wheeled Nizhoni and clapped against the gray flanks with his heels. The horse lurched away in an easy, flopping jog.

She kicked the bay angrily and followed Linc as an obedient lamb falls in behind its ewe, for she had no more choice in the matter than did a suckling. She had no idea where she was nor where John's camp might lie, other than it obviously lay in a more or less northerly direction. The chill wind told her Linc's weather prognostications were right. Did he know that cold now cut into her so deeply? Did he care? She snorted.

She kept her mind off the discomfort of her legs and

backside by dreaming up applicable adjectives for this boorish man. *Coarse. Insensitive. Uncouth. Unable to distinguish right from wrong (Just think of his comment about her precious body! Indeed!). Irritating. Terribly irritating. Uncultured. Uneducated. Inconsiderate. Uncouth.* No, she'd already said *uncouth.*

Then again, for a second time he had literally saved her from a fate worse than death, and quite likely from death itself. Hurting Dasanie bothered him immensely, though she could not see why. Dasanie was clearly the wrongdoer, yet Linc acted as if she were somehow responsible. Apparently he simply did not understand the necessity of virtue.

She was grateful, of course, that he had been following her (and again she could not guess why he bothered). She was grateful that he interceded on her behalf. She wished only that he might be easier to understand. She understood John. They thought alike, she and John.

Didn't they?

CHAPTER 8

DARKNESS CAME, AND with it that disorientation that had so terrified Naomi before. Only the fact that Linc obviously knew where he was going kept her from panicking anew. The hills and shrubs and spindly, low trees dissolved from shades of gray to shades of black. The sky was black and thick. They rode from darkness into darkness, swimming a black sea.

She asked "How long yet?" several times. Each response was "About three hours," regardless of the time that had elapsed since the last time she asked. She quit asking.

A cold wet feather touched her cheek, lingered, and was gone. Another brushed her lips. A third stung as it touched the welt on her cheek. She heard Nizhoni ahead but could not see him. The wet feathers came faster. They stuck to her eyebrows, paused on her nose. What amazing country, this desert! Here was snow, yet the sun burned harsh enough to make her nose peel. At least this snow was much safer for her than rain. She got cold, but she stayed rather dry. She pulled her torn cape closer around, trying to keep the ragged ends together.

Ever since that anguished cry to God for help, she had not really thought to commune with Him. She was shocked to realize she had not even thanked Him for this latest deliverance. An even worse jolt was the realization of the part Linc Rawlins had again played in her deliverance, of the way his appearance had coincided exactly with her plea to God. She mended the oversight immediately.

"Linc?"

"About three hours yet."

"It occurred to me just now that when I asked God for help, He helped. Unfortunately I didn't remember to thank Him until just now. Which I've done . . ."

"Good."

"However, I see that twice now you have been an instrument of God in my behalf. You're quite literally an answer to prayer, you know. You must have a marvelous relationship with God yourself, to be so ready to answer His beck and call. To respond so effectively as His servant."

A cold, derisive little chuckle floated back to her through the darkness.

She kicked her bay to catch up. She wanted to be closer, better to hear the nuances of his voice. "Why are you laughing? It's true!"

Nizhoni nickered and broke into a noisy jog. Her own horse sighed and quickened his pace to keep up. If this pace continued long, she would bounce right out of the saddle altogether. She was just about getting the rhythm when her horse came to a halt.

The sheepskin collar loomed waist-high beside her. "We're there. Down you go."

At last! She could not bend her knees the way she wanted them to go. With great difficulty she swung one leg up onto her horse's rump. It stuck there.

Linc chuckled in the darkness. An arm wrapped around

her waist and roughly dragged her to the ground. At first her legs refused to support her at all, but that powerful arm did.

She straightened, hanging onto the saddle, and breathed deeply. "Thank you. I believe I am ambulatory now."

The arm and the collar dissolved into the darkness. Wood scraped on wood. A match hissed. He stood in a doorway framed by massive timbers.

"Mi casa es su casa." My house is yours—the standard Spanish greeting. Was he fluent in Spanish or was that simply a phrase he had picked up, just as she had? He touched his match to a candle stub and walked inside. From the candle he lighted a small coal oil lamp on a table across the room.

She hobbled inside on fence-post legs. The building was a huge, single, octagonal room. She was inside a Navajo hogan. She had seen many hogans, but never had she stood inside one. Somehow she expected a few mats and gaudy blankets on which to sit and sleep, perhaps an open fire in the middle, and a general climate of squalor. This was nothing at all like her wild imaginings.

"You have furniture!" It blurted out of her.

He looked at her a moment, bemused. The eyes tilted. "Disappointed that you don't have to sit on the floor?"

"Not at all. I'm sorry, I didn't mean to . . ." She bit her lip. "It's clean and neat and very homey. I compliment you."

In the middle of the room squatted a little iron wood-stove. Its stovepipe seemed outsized for so modest a stove. It rose from the back of the stove a foot or two, elbowed out across the room another yard, then shot straight up through the center of the roof. He must have laid his kindling and wood before he left. He dropped to one knee in front of the opened stove door, tossed in a match, twirled the damper discs, and trotted out the door.

She stood by the stove and looked around more carefully. The far end was obviously a food preparation area with heavy oak chairs and a table. Open shelves and a curtained cupboard stood along the wall. And behind her there was the sleeping space. Of three narrow little beds along the wall, two were made up with blankets. The third was simply a lumpy burlap mattress on a crude wooden frame.

She carried one of the heavy chairs to the stove and sat down. Already the iron sides were warming up. She really should go out and help with the horses, but she couldn't move. The fire crackled and whistled and made the dampers rattle.

Twenty minutes later Linc popped back inside, laden with bedroll and saddlebags. "Fire catch?"

"Feels wonderful," she nodded. She felt sleepy sitting up.

He tossed the bedroll on the farthest bed, lugged the saddlebags to the table, and shook the snow off his bulky collar. It must be coming down thickly out there. He dumped the saddlebags and began lining up cans and sacks and packets on the shelves.

She stood up, barely able to flex anything, and tottered over to him. "Excuse me . . . but when I suggested that you're God's servant, you laughed. Does that mean you believe in the Navajo gods and spirits?"

"Some, when I was young. Not any more. I don't bother them and they don't bother me."

"Oh." She considered that a moment. "Surely, though, you don't feel that way about God. The supreme God, I mean."

"Why not? He's never done me any special favors, and I haven't done Him any that I know of. And that includes shepherding you." He held up a little tin. "You like beef?"

"Yes, yes, beef is fine." She was eager to get on with the

discussion. "But God is the one Person—the only Person —in heaven or earth who is worthy of worship. Not for what He'll do for you; simply for His own sake. The Indian spirits don't merit full devotion, but because of His nature, He does. It's not a matter of swapping favors with some divine chum."

"My father was six feet four. That's exactly Lincoln's height. And he was dark-haired and skinny—like Lincoln. Abe was his ideal, his hero, his commander-in-chief, during the war. Pa was proud of the resemblance and I think he pictured me as a junior-grade Honest Abe. He was enthusiastic about education; it meant a lot to Pa because Lincoln worked so hard to educate himself. I was halfway through third grade when Pa died. Ma pulled me out of school that same day, and I never went back."

"Yes, but . . . ?"

"She figured I'd hear often enough how I was an ignorant breed—didn't need the schoolmaster telling me too. Besides, I could read and write and cipher pretty good by then. Good enough to get by. She took over my education and taught me the Indian ways. But it was too late. Too much of Pa had rubbed off on me already."

"Yes, but what has that to do with the Christian faith?"

He plunked the last can on the shelf. "Pa was a Christian because Lincoln was. Pa and Lincoln—the white ways. Ma—the Indian ways. They don't mix, either of them. Not the schooling, not the gods, not anything. I got 'em both in me, like oil and water, and I'm not big enough to hold all that. I don't fit in peaked houses and I don't fit in this roundhouse. And neither of the gods fit me."

"But that's so . . . so . . . conciliatory. So defeatist. Unvictorious. We're called to live victoriously and . . . it's very sad," she sighed.

"I get by. Stuff some more wood on the fire, will you?"

She hobbled to the stove. "So what are you going to do? Just drift in one end of life and out the other?"

"It's worked so far." He stirred things into a pan, a handful of this and a handful of that. When he spoke, he seemed to be talking mostly to himself. "Been thinking though. If I find some good reason to go, was thinking I might wander up to Alberta, Canada. I hear they don't much care who your parents are so long as you're a good farmer. My pa had one of the nicest little places on the Arkansas River. He really knew his stuff. And I picked up a few things about herding and ranching here in Arizona. Spent some time down in Patagonia."

"Patagonia. You mean Arizona territory, of course, not Argentina."

"I'm a traveling man, but not that far." His voice lilted cheerfully. His defeatist attitude didn't seem to bother him in the least.

It bothered her immensely, and that confused her. Why should she care anyway? True, his was a lost soul, and she must care about that because God did. But everything seemed so confusing.

She slammed the iron stove door and stood up. Her legs would never forgive her those days in the saddle. "Do you suppose Joe Dasanie will follow us here to get his horse back? Or get even? Or both?"

Linc's cheerful face slipped behind a dark cloud. "He has to hole up and stay dry if he's gonna survive. By the time he's moving again, the rain and snow will have wiped out our trail. He won't have anything to follow. He won't be here."

"But he will join his partner in crime again. That Neeskah. We really must go warn John!"

"Assuming Dasanie lives. He's a tough bird, so he prob'ly will. Yeah, I guess we'll head north when the

69

weather clears. I suspect we have a good three-day blow whipping around our ears here."

"Three days?!" The thought startled her. Three days! She had considered it improper to travel with the unmarried John Carter, and in his camp she lived in a separate tent with Felicidad as something of a chaperone. Now here she sat, condemned to living in the same room for three days with an exceedingly eligible and, yes, good-looking bachelor— probably an amoral one too. The very thought of it shamed her. "I don't suppose there are any other buildings nearby where I might, ah, stay."

"Got the hay shed out by the corral, but it's just a roof with no sides. A ramada. You'd get kinda cold. And there's the one-holer out behind, if you don't mind sleeping sitting up."

He was making fun of her. Worse, he was making fun of her high standards of behavior. The stove sides were cherry red now, uncomfortably warm at close quarters. She moved her chair a few feet further away and plunked down on it, so irritated by his impudence and crude references that she dared not speak.

"Which reminds me." He brought two pans over and set them on the stove. "I ran a rope between the door here and the outhouse. Keep the rope in your hand all the way out and all the way back, even if you think you can see. The wind whips up the snow now and then and blinds you when you aren't expecting it. You can get lost ten feet from the door and wander off. Whiteouts don't have directions."

She glanced at the three narrow wooden beds. They stood right next to each other. Briefly she remembered Dasanie's reaching, flailing, groping hand. If his lust had flamed in that cold and sterile wilderness, what would this warm, intimate atmosphere do for Linc's desires? Their very proximity was a dangerous temptation. She closed her eyes against the memory of Dasanie's chilling leer.

She muttered, mostly to herself, "Perhaps we could fashion some sort of partition out of bed linen. Hang it from the rafters up there, or . . . But then I don't know how . . ." Her eyes were hot. "There must be some way to obtain privacy. Perhaps . . ." Scalding tears poised on the rims of her eyelids. There would be no privacy, no escape from this man's presence. The tears brimmed over and boiled down her cheeks. She couldn't see, and her nose plugged up instantly.

A chair clunked down beside her. A long arm wrapped around her shoulders. "It really bothers you, doesn't it? It's not just appearances."

"Everything is so wrong!" she sobbed. "The more I try to do things right, the worse they get! I feel so lost and confused. I pray to God for help and, instead, I get *you*." She shuddered and looked up at him quickly. "Oh, I don't mean that—not that way. I'm sorry. It's just that—well, when I asked God to help, I didn't exactly envision you. You're really very nice, and I'm grateful." She was caught in another spasm of sobbing. "But here we are stuck in the same room for three whole days . . . and I don't . . ."

He tipped her head against his shoulder and massaged her throbbing temple. His touch was soft and comforting and gentle. "Listen. We'll fix up something so you can have your privacy. It's all right. And it won't be all that bad anyway. I'll be spending a lot of time outside—minding the horses, splitting wood and stuff. The woodpile was low when I left, and I think Doli probably borrowed some more while I was gone. I hope you can meet Doli sometime. She's like you in a couple ways. Except she's Navajo. And she has this little boy."

For lack of a handkerchief, her hands and face were all wet. She took a deep breath. "I don't know why I'm crying like this. You should be the one crying. At least I know what's moral and refined even if I can't always hold to the appearance of it. You're so . . . so . . . I can't think of the word I want. *Depraved* certainly isn't it. Anyway, you're so lost you don't even know what's morally right and wrong. I have expectations. I can look forward to doing well when I reach San Francisco. You have nothing at all to look forward to. I have a true, dependable, loving God. You refuse to believe in Him. Your state is far worse than mine.''

His broad hands tipped her face up so he could look her in the eye. ''You're not just wallowing around in self-pity. You really do care about me.''

''Oh, well, uh, no. I don't really care about you *that* way. It's just, uh . . . well, God loves you enough to let His Son die to pay for your sins, you see. So I should care too. Please don't misunderstand. It's not romantic. It's . . . it's doctrinal.''

''It's delightful.'' His dark eyes smiled. She studied the happy little tilt to his eyes. They were not oriental eyes with the almond shape, nor were they the shape you find in people as a general rule. The eyes were simply indescribable, with their crinkly corners constantly and naturally posed in an attitude of cheerful bemusement.

He drew her in against himself and cradled her head as one would comfort a child with a skinned knee. She snuggled against him, grateful for this warm, close respite from a cold world.

He rubbed her shoulder and purred, avuncular. ''It'll be all right. You don't have to worry about your reputation. The only way anyone'll know you were here will be if you tell them. So don't tell anyone. I won't. Your appearance will stay as stiff and starched as you care to keep it. And you're safe as far as I'm concerned too. Not that you aren't pretty enough . . .''

She shivered, yet she was not cold. She felt herself drifting off to sleep in spite of herself.

He straightened and removed his arm. "I have some old blankets stashed somewhere around here. May have to darn some holes if the mice've got to them. We'll divide the house here into many mansions. You'll have your privacy."

In my Father's house are many mansions. That was John 14:1. No, it was John 14:2. Linc was quoting Jesus directly. This man who swore no allegiance to God knew God's Word well enough to allude to it. On purpose? She was beginning to think every word he spoke had some purpose, if only to himself privately. Puzzling. Intriguing. She wished her sleepy mind were alert enough to consider this. Obviously, he was much better read than three-and-a-half years of school would indicate.

Was he trustworthy? So far it seemed so.

Even so, it didn't make this questionable situation right. It was going to be a very long three days.

CHAPTER 9

NAOMI REMEMBERED HOW quickly snow became soiled in northwestern Ohio where she grew up. Cows and horses sullied the white blankets of their pastures. They churned the snow into the dirt of their barnyards. Sheep and hogs rooted in it, spoiling it beyond repair. Wagons and carriages cut it up, sleighs sliced through it. Then the snowplows would render the final foul stroke by disarranging its plump smoothness into lumpy welts.

She settled carefully into the saddle and gazed out over the unbroken whiteness stretching across this mesa. Their horses would cut a thin and barely visible line across the snow. That was all. Its vastness would remain unscarred until it finally melted back into the bold colors of the desert. She liked pristine snow like this, particularly when the air was so warm. Here was lovely snow with none of the discomfort of clammy cold. Already the morning sun was suggesting she remove her cape.

Linc came out of the hogan and closed the door carefully behind him. "Got everything?"

She nodded. "I double-checked. A lot of snow fell. Almost a foot."

He swung aboard Nizhoni without touching the stirrups. "Unusual. Guess it wants to go out with a bang. Last snow of the winter."

"That's what you said before."

Linc urged Nizhoni out into the sun-brilliant whiteness. "Gotta be right one of these times."

Her horse fell in behind, extended its neck and plodded with its ears flopping. "Are you sure we won't be too late? Maybe those two are doing their mischief right now."

"Dasanie said they were gonna jump Carter soon as he found gold, right?"

"That's what he said."

"Then your bone-digger's safe. He won't find any gold in that country. All sedimentary, no quartz intrusions. Now further south and west—Prescott, Wickenburg, the river —there, he'd be in danger. He might accidentally stumble onto gold while hunting his old bones, and whammy, they'd get him!"

She urged her horse closer. "Are you making sport of me again?"

He smiled. His lips said, "Never," but his eyes twinkled and said, "Every chance I get."

"How do you know all that anyway?" She had no idea whether he might be stringing out a whopping lie. It did sound authentic.

"Who made all the money when Tombstone and Bisbee boomed?"

"The undertakers, if half the stories I heard are true. Not the miners, I'll wager."

"Right. Farmers, green grocers and the assay office. I worked at the assay office one winter in Bisbee. Couldn't ride 'til my broken leg healed up. Broke up samples, mixed

75

acid, and read every book the assayer had in the place."

"Geology books."

"Even some paleontology stuff like your John fancies."

She frowned. "Are you one of those evolutionists?"

"That's natural history. The books didn't have much in that line. You know the fossil series the evolutionists talk about was put together thirty years before your Charles Darwin, over in England. Cambrian, Ordovician. That stuff."

"He's not *my* Charles Darwin." Naomi felt suddenly uncomfortable and it took several minutes for her to decide why. Linc was talking like a college-educated geologist. He knew more about John's field of interest than she did, yet John had regaled her with salient points of paleontology for hours on end. She had established in her mind that Linc was uneducated and now he was proving her wrong. It irked her and unsettled her. She had best change the subject altogether. "How did you break your leg?"

"Riding a horse that didn't want to be rode, down south of Tubac." He stopped so abruptly her horse threw its head up to avoid colliding with Nizhoni. Linc was peering far out across the rolling white mesa top. They were not the only persons to blemish the faultless snow. A team and wagon was approaching from the northeast. A woman's voice called faintly.

Linc leaned forward slightly. Nizhoni lunged and was off at a dead run toward the wagon. Naomi relinquished control of her horse and simply hung on as it followed.

The wagoner was a Navajo woman Naomi's age or a bit older. Her broad brown face was tight with worry. She babbled to Linc as he pulled alongside and never so much as noticed Naomi.

Linc swung Nizhoni around to the rear of the wagon and slid off. "You might as well tie your horse here too. Ride on a nice flat seat while you may."

"Tie my horse? Where are we going?"

"This is Doli. Her son just got hurt in a hunting accident. We're going over to her place."

She slid off her horse. "But what about John?"

"He's a big boy. Doli's son is a little boy; needs help more."

"But . . ."

But Linc was already hopping up into the wagon. He spoke to the woman in that nasal speech. She nodded vigorously and handed him the lines. They traded places, Linc taking her seat, as Naomi climbed in. The woman motioned; Naomi was to sit beside Linc. Indian etiquette probably required that Naomi politely decline, but her suffering backside decreed otherwise. She scrambled into the seat as Linc swung the team around.

All during that snowstorm (which was a two-day blow and not the three-day affair he had predicted), Linc had dutifully kept his distance. He had puttered about the kitchen area or worked outside. Once he had brought in a fistful of tail hairs from the corral and spent hours braiding them into a long, elaborate plait with knots and loops. It was a bosal, he said, but she had no idea what that might be. It seemed, when he held it up for her, to be a substitute for a horse's bridle. She had returned to the privacy of a curtained apartment by night and also occasionally during the day. She slept with her clothes on and suspected, but was not sure, that he did also. Never in those confined hours had he come near her or made any sort of untoward comment or suggestion. In every way, the whole time, he had behaved like a perfect gentleman.

How strange—now that she was sitting beside him in this jouncy, springy wagon seat, abroad on a sprawling mesa with only snow and sky—she felt his closeness and it excited her. She remembered John's kiss and the feelings it had awakened. Now, perversely, she was keenly aware of Linc who was so near their arms brushed. She could hear him breathe sometimes when he leaned against her on a curve. She wanted to cling to him and to feel his male strength, but she dared not.

They rattled up to a hogan much like Linc's. It must not have snowed as much in this area. The snow was thin and already melted away in spots. Linc hopped down and ran inside. He closed the door behind him.

The woman stood at Naomi's shoulder, gripping the seat back. Her mouth formed a tight line. Her eyes crinkled hard and black like chips of coal.

Linc stuck his head out and spoke in Navajo. He glanced at Naomi. "I just told her her hogan is still a good place to be." He disappeared back inside.

The woman's steely composure melted like the snow in her dooryard. The mouth trembled; the eyes dissolved. She clapped her hand over her mouth and cheek and sobbed. Was she crying from grief or from relief? Naomi could not tell.

Naomi would not sit meekly by and play the outsider. She climbed over the wagon wheel and splacked down into the wet dirt. She pushed inside through the heavy door. The hogan was dark but for a single candle. Linc had seated himself beside a low pallet on the floor near the door, his grasshopper legs folded up tight. He was mumbling in casual conversation with a small boy who was lying there.

The child was much younger than Naomi had anticipated. He could not be more than nine years old, even if he were small for his age. His left side and armpit were a bloody mess.

Linc glanced up at her. "You wearing a petticoat?"

"What?"

78

"Can I have it? Doli ran out of bandages. He keeps soaking through dressings. I need your petticoat."

What could she say? To refuse would hardly be an act of Christian charity. She stepped behind him as far as possible and loosened the tie string up under her skirts. Her petticoat dropped to the floor. She took it over to him. "This is a bit irregular."

"This whole month has been irregular."

"You can say that again. Can I help?"

"I think we about have it here. Stick around. Doli will be in soon, once she gets herself back together. She's a widow, and Kee here is her only child. That makes him special."

Somehow that bit of information gave her no comfort. The term "widow" had such a predatory connotation when applied to a woman so young. "Doli's not very old to be a widow. Recent?"

"Year ago, little more."

"Illness?"

"Raiders. Her husband was protecting their flock. Doli lost her man and her sheep both."

Naomi knew that in this culture a flock was tantamount to the family jewels, the family wealth. "It never occurred to me that outlaws would steal from Indians."

His face tightened. "Dineh raiding Dineh. When the army rounded up the Navajos, they missed a lot of the really bad eggs. But internment worked, from the Anglos' point of view. The Dineh came home peaceable. They're careful to keep their fingers off the Anglos or anything the Anglos own. Whites left 'em alone, except for some missionaries and the Indian school business."

"And the bad eggs who never really fit into the tribe. Right?"

"Right. They don't dare raid Anglos, and the Dineh despise 'em. There are still a couple bands of them, even after

79

all these years. They prey on Dineh, other tribes, and Mexicans occasionally. If they ever cut loose on Anglos, the whole Navajo reservation will go up in flames. Anglos will take revenge on everybody, not just the outlaws."

"Aren't there any Indian army protectors of some sort? Warriors to handle the raiders?"

"Not really. That's why Doli's been talking about moving. She has distant relatives of some sort up around Keet Seel. Better for her than sitting here. Raiders learn about a woman living alone here . . ." His voice trailed off.

"A long journey for a woman alone."

In a fatherly gesture Linc poked a shaggy lock of hair out of Kee's face. "She'd have company part of the way, at least. Local elders are talking about moving the whole clan north to Moenkopi. They're fed up losing sheep and sometimes lives. Doubt anyone really wants to go, but what can they do?"

There he was with that defeatist attitude again. Frustrating! And it wasn't even any of her business.

Kee shuddered and squirmed deeper into his covers. He was drifting asleep by degrees.

"You said a hunting accident. Isn't he terribly little to be out hunting?"

"He's the man of the family. The same kind of accident happens to grown men plenty of times. His hunting partner's shotgun went off when they were working rabbits. Here. Hold this."

She anchored one end of what had recently been her undergarment as he wrapped and tucked. His hands moved firmly, gently, gracefully. She thought about how comforting they felt when he held her close that night. In fact, he seemed to be treating this boy about the same way he had treated her. Why had she broken down in tears then? Even if they came only from weariness, she regretted the incident.

Linc grinned at the boy and spoke. The boy opened his eyes, managed a feeble smile, and replied. His huge eyes rolled toward Naomi and he asked a question.

Linc replied. His tone of voice and the child's sudden grin suggested they were sharing some snide comment at Naomi's expense. Why did she feel persecuted? Because she was an alien here; that was why. And neither of these people (nor Doli either, for that matter) was trying in the least to put Naomi at ease. She began to appreciate, at least a tiny bit, the feelings Linc must harbor when he felt he fit in nowhere.

Doli came inside a few minutes later. Without looking at Naomi, she stoked her stove and set a pot on it. Naomi sighed. Apparently they were staying for dinner. She wanted to be on her way to John and here she sat, for all practical purposes, in a foreign country. Even worse, she felt like just another piece of furniture, unnoticed and unneeded.

From somewhere outside came a faint, gentle lowing. She knew that sound. She pushed the door open and stepped out into dazzling sun. She waited a few moments for her eyes to adjust. The lowing sound came from the corral. She walked over through the melting slop and peered over the chest-high corral poles. A scrawny, bedraggled brown cow peered back at her. The cow's udder bulged and sagged.

"You haven't been milked at all today, have you? You poor old thing. Very well. At least it's something to do." She walked over to the shed, her shoes making slushing sounds in the muck. There was the milk pail, all dented and dirty. No milking stool? Here was a rough spool of stovewood, unsplit. She carried the pail and the round back to the corral and climbed over the fence.

The cow mooed, almost a question. Naomi rubbed behind its ears and behind its flaking horns, under the baggy jowls and along the top of its neck. She scratched her way down the neck and across the cow's bony back to the flanks. She plunked the round of wood in the mud and settled herself precariously; it was not a stable seat. If this cow moved about much or kicked, someone else could milk her.

Naomi pressed her head into the cow's flank and stroked a teat. She tucked the pail between her knees and took up a second teat. She drew gently, hesitantly; it had been years since she had milked a cow. Had she forgotten how, or was the cow holding back? She pressed her fists upward with each stroke, deep into the udder.

A thin, colorless stream drummed against the bottom of the pail. Here it came. Naomi had lost none of her old touch. The cow was letting her milk down now. The milk came watery-gray at first and now creamy white. Naomi often wondered why you could not simply shake a cow, as you would shake a bottle of separated milk, to bring down a more uniform product.

The milk splashed into the pail. Foam billowed halfway up the sides. The fresh, warm smell of new milk—that unique and glorious aroma—surrounded Naomi and bathed her in memories of home and childhood.

But she was no longer accustomed to such chores, and her fingers were growing tired. She crooked her thumbs under for a better grip, as her mother did. Her mother's hands might be crippled by arthritis, but she was still the best milkmaid in Lucas County.

In fact, her mother was the best everything in Lucas County. She painstakingly weeded her cabbages by hand because, she claimed, cabbages don't like to be bothered while they're growing. Her cabbages always took first place at the fair. Her cherry pies took prizes, too, and her white bread always won in its division until Naomi began entering her own.

Naomi smiled. She pictured her mother climbing into their sour-cherry tree every summer to pick cherries—and falling out of the tree at least once every summer. Naomi must have spent two years of her life—the time not spent milking—pitting pie cherries.

Naomi sniffled. Her nose was plugged up again. Why was she smiling through tears? They were streaming down her cheeks and dripping into the milk. There were no farms in Arizona even remotely similar to the farm back home. She wanted to feel green grass under her feet again. She wanted to hear tree leaves rustle overhead.

She was drawing pure cream now. She kept an eye out and watched the cow's tail, lest the old bossy grow restless and kick the pail over. There seemed no need to fear. The cow stood complacently with its eyes half-closed.

She sniffed again and wiped her eyes on her upper arms. The tears were leaving as mysteriously as they had arrived. She stripped the cow thoroughly and felt a surge of disappointment when nothing more would come.

Reluctantly she stood up with her pail. She scratched the cow again behind the horns. "I enjoyed our time together very much. Thank you, whatever your name is."

"Chil Abee."

She wheeled, nearly dropping the milk.

Linc leaned casually across the top rail, watching her.

"How long have you been here?"

He shrugged. "Awhile. You might like yard-long words and fancy speech, but you're a farm girl underneath it all."

"My father owns four hundred acres of prime bottom land along the Maumee River near Toledo. I was milking when I was five." She handed him the pail and retrieved her makeshift stool from the mud.

He was opening a gate she hadn't even noticed. She slogged over to it and stepped out onto firmer ground.

"Why'd you leave? Don't like farming?" He took the chunk of wood and tossed it toward the woodpile.

"I like farming very much. But I, well, I like a more sophisticated lifestyle even better."

"Now that you're educated, farming's not good enough for you."

"That's not it at all!" She would have picked up the pail, but he did. "I have four older brothers; so I wouldn't get much of the farm even if I stayed. I just . . . I don't know. I just wanted to come west—to see what it's like and maybe . . ."

"Wanderlust. What's the fancy word you used?"

"Peripatetic. But that's not exactly it either."

He set the milk down in snow on the shady side of the hogan. "Well, if you ever decide to quit peripatizing and settle down, you'll make a pretty good farm wife."

"I'll make an even better teacher of arts and languages, thank you." She hesitated, uncertain how to phrase this next thought. "Understand I am in no way ashamed of farming. But it's a part of my life that is past. In the distant past, after all these years. I'd just as soon it was not discussed with the general public, so to speak."

"You don't want me to tell your professor you milk cows."

She felt her cheeks getting warm. "He's a city man. He doesn't know or care anything about country people, and I don't want him to . . . I just think . . ."

"Don't give me that line about not being ashamed." His eyes, no longer smiling, were boring into hers. "You know, I was starting to admire you till you spoiled it right there." He turned and walked around the side of the hogan. She heard the door scrape and close.

She stepped out into the sun. It was as warm as summer now; the snow had nearly all fled. Blue sky arched unbroken from horizon to horizon. She yearned for the closeness of Ohio's forests, and, yes, even for the frequent overcast of Ohio skies. The tears were creeping back.

She didn't care that they were returning. She didn't care a bit.

CHAPTER 10

NAOMI STEPPED OUT INTO the golden evening light and closed the door of Doli's hogan behind her. She looked in vain for snow. The only whiteness left lay in the deep shadows of the hogan and corral. She was glad dinner was over. Doli spoke rarely and then only one or two syllables to Linc. Kee just lay there. Linc said nothing, but then he rarely said anything. And when he spoke, it was usually to Doli—in Navajo. Depressing.

What was John doing now? Was he still safe? She thought of that kiss again and found herself looking forward to the next one. Next one? That was being a bit presumptuous, was it not? She smiled to herself. So be it.

The door scraped and Linc came wandering out to stand beside her. He squinted in the bright light; his eyes pinched down, then opened again to their usual unique tilt.

He smiled at her. "You doing all right?"

"My feet and shoes are soaked, but that's become the norm of late. I'm doing as well as can be expected for a poor little foreigner with no grasp of the native language."

"Navajo takes some getting used to. Doesn't behave the way English or Spanish does."

"The only syllables I recognized as being repeated were *nah* and *gay*. What's *nah-gay?*"

"*Naguey*. The Navajo name my mother gave me."

"So that's you. Now I know two words. *Naguey* and *hogan*. Wonderful. Oh, and *nizhoni*. Pretty."

"*Nizhoni* isn't exactly the same as pretty in English. It's 'a pretty thing.' Now, 'a pretty place' is *hozhoni*."

"*Hozhoni*. Hogan. *Ho* is place?"

"*Hogan*. Home place. *Nigan,* your home. *Shigan*. My home. *Shigandi*. At my home. See? Nothing to it."

"You're right about one thing; it certainly doesn't behave like English. When we first arrived, you told Doli her hogan was a pretty place to be, or something like that."

"If a person dies inside a hogan, unless he's very very old and dies quietly of natural causes, his ghost is there."

"So if Kee were dead when you went inside, the hogan would be haunted?"

"Sort of. Then you call it *Ho-kee-gan*. Doli would move out and let Kee have the place." He thought a few moments. "You asked me about Navajo spirits and the Anglo God, remember? I forget the question exactly."

"I remember: You subscribe to neither God nor spirits."

"I found the hogan where I'm staying now pretty much the way you saw it. Furnished. In good repair. Solid roof. It's almost certain someone left it because someone else died in it, and recently, too. *Ho-kee-gan*. A good Navajo wouldn't come near the place except maybe to burn it, out of fear and respect for the dead." He gestured helplessly. "I moved right in. I know the beliefs—the traditions—and it doesn't bother me."

"So you're not a good Navajo. I see. You sound rather like an empty one."

He stared at her. "An empty one." He broke off the stare and let his eyes drift toward the horizon. Should she speak, or was he wrapping himself up in some deep thought? He frowned and shaded his eyes. "Now who's this?"

A small boy was trudging toward them out of the distance. He kept his eyes on the ground, and he seemed to slow up as he approached.

Linc pointed out the other way, across the corral. "It's not polite to watch someone coming."

John had said that; she remembered now. But she didn't say that. "You seem determined to imbue me with the Navajo language and culture."

"Just trying to make you feel at home."

"I doubt anything can do that. When will we get back on the road, as if there were a road in this wilderness? Back to Mr. Carter?"

"I don't know. We'll see how Kee's doing tomorrow. If he doesn't develop too much of a fever and infection overnight, we'll leave."

"Mmm." That was not a particularly satisfactory answer.

The boy was strolling into the yard here now. He was about Kee's size, and he looked for all the world as though he wished he were in Florida. He carried two dead jackrabbits by the ears.

Linc spoke pleasantly.

The boy mumbled a reply and stared at the mud.

Linc pushed the door open and said something. The boy shuffled inside, his eyes still downcast. Linc and Naomi followed him into the hogan.

Without lifting his eyes, the boy extended the rabbits at arm's length. Doli accepted them and spoke. He shook his head, more a sorry wag than a firm denial. He nodded at her next comment. Like a whipped dog he shuffled over to the pallet and to Kee.

How Naomi wished she understood Navajo, if only for this one occasion! Linc followed the boy over to Kee and flopped down casually by the pallet. He manipulated the boy as a potter shapes clay. He lectured sternly, cajoled lightly, conversed earnestly. The boy's hangdog expression brightened to concern and thence to equally earnest conversation. Five minutes later he and Kee were both grinning and telling Linc some lengthy anecdote filled with babbling boy-sounds and wild gestures.

Linc described something, apparently a place. The little visitor hopped up and ran outside. Moments later he returned with a small wrapped parcel. Naomi remembered Linc stuffing that very package in his saddlebag this morning with a curt comment, "Just in case I meet some friends."

With elaborate pomp, Linc unwrapped it. He held up a red lollipop and at the visitor's behest handed it to Kee. The next was yellow. The visitor accepted it, hesitated, then spoke. Linc replied in no uncertain terms and wrapped the remaining candies up securely. The visitor left presently —with the parcel.

Perhaps now Naomi would feel less estranged. Perhaps Doli even spoke English and simply had neglected so far to do so. Linc came wandering over to the stove, so Naomi ended up there also. He reached for the coffeepot and poured himself a cup. He rumbled something in Navajo. Doli replied and handed him a second coffee mug. He held it out toward Naomi.

"Like a cup?"

"Thank you." It disturbed her immensely that this Doli continued to exclude her—even in so small a matter. In fact, from the moment Linc stepped through the door, it was as though he were the master of this house. "You seem to get on quite well with children. I assume our young visitor is the aforementioned hunting partner."

Linc nodded. "Yep. He pulled the trigger. Took plenty of courage for him to come here after something like that. He didn't know if Kee was alive or dead when he knocked on the door. His mother raised him well."

Naomi cocked her head, impressed. "And what was the business with the candy?"

Linc laughed. "He has courage, but he's also a coyote. He asked me to give him three extras to take home to his three brothers. I happen to know his brothers are two thousand miles away in the school at Carlisle. His family are all coyotes."

She stared at her coffee awhile. It was too hot to drink. "What's his name? You never said."

"His parents changed his name a couple years ago. It's 'The Dog' now."

"You can't be serious!"

Linc was refilling his cup already. "You asked why Dasanie might be so bitter. Try this. The Indian agent wanted to send The Dog's brothers to the boarding school in Carlisle. To Pennsylvania. Their parents said no; they needed the boys at home. But they had these two daughters who are a little muddled upstairs. The girls can't learn quick, have trouble thinking things through. They're too irresponsible to be trusted with the flocks. The parents figured maybe the school could help the girls learn how to think. Learn how to learn."

"That sounds reasonable. A disciplined mind."

"Well, the agent only wanted the smartest kids—to make the school look better. One morning the three boys go out with the flock. The next day a neighbor finds the sheep scattered all over, untended. The agent had kidnapped the

90

boys and sent them off to the school. Tied 'em up, put 'em on the train.''

"I agree that's certainly not the way to go about it. But . . .''

"The parents have a big flock. The Dog's too young to herd them full time and the girls can't. So what are the parents going to do now?''

"I see where that would work a hardship. But . . . but education is very important. The world is changing, and education can . . .''

"Sure. That's what my father said. Kee here is getting an education. He's learning to read and write and cipher and speak English. Goes to school sometimes, and I've been helping him. Tutoring. He's learning just fine. He doesn't have to go to Carlisle. Can you imagine what would happen to Doli if her special son got carted off?''

Naomi needed time to think and she had no time. "Yes, but . . .''

"Anyway, that's why The Dog's parents changed his name. His brothers are doing pretty good back there, apparently. So the agent's been coming around and asking if there's any more at home. The parents tell him the truth: 'No one here except the two girls and The Dog.' ''

"I'm sorry. I'm sure you're telling the Indian side of it, but I can't believe you're being totally honest. Rather, totally objective. I'm sure there must be . . . I mean . . .''

"What I'm telling you is why Joe Dasanie might have a fight to pick with Anglos. Just about everyone has a similar story. That kind of stuff goes on constantly.'' He drained his cup and spoke to Doli. She handed him the two rabbits. He took them out the door.

Doli chopped onions and peppers, but her mind seemed far removed from her work. Was it the onions or the circumstances that brought tears to her eyes? Now and then she would glance over at the sleeping Kee. She paid her guest no notice. She dumped a bowlful of chopped vegetables into a stew pot—tomorrow's dinner, apparently—put more wood in the stove and flung a blanket over her shoulders. She walked outside without so much as looking at Naomi.

The door was ajar. Naomi did not deliberately eavesdrop, of course; that's not polite. But from the doorway she could admire the last throes of a lovely sunset. And there were Linc and Doli over by the corral. Linc had gutted and skinned the rabbits. Now he hung the scrawny carcasses from a corral rail.

Doli's black wool skirt contrasted starkly with the weathered fence poles and seemed to blend into the wet dirt at her feet. She stood talking a few moments, then melted against him with her head on his chest. Naomi thought of his gentle, comforting touch. Doli had picked the right place to find solace; Linc was very good at that sort of thing. Now he was holding her close, folded in those arms, brushing his fingertips across her cheek and through the long black hair. It was all very brotherly.

But the kiss was not at all brotherly. He kissed her, casually at first, then intensely. They became so thoroughly impassioned Naomi marveled that the mud did not begin to steam around their feet. Eventually their lips parted. Doli giggled at some mumbled comment. They wandered, arms entwined, back toward the hay shed and out of sight.

Disgusted, Naomi stepped back and closed the door. She was alone in a dark, stuffy, cornerless room but for a slumbering child. And while she languished in moody isolation, those two were . . . were . . . disgusting! Perhaps their relationship was not so sordid as it appeared. Perhaps they were right this minute walking out behind the hogan to enjoy the last glimmers of evening light. Nonsense! She knew exactly what they were doing now. Well, maybe only in general terms. She had no first-hand knowledge of exactly what goes on in a thoroughly intimate relationship. But then again, perhaps they were . . . ?

She remembered a sermon a pastor in Santa Fe had delivered. His theme was an exposition on the immorality of the pagan Apaches in that area, and thereby a demonstration that they were all of the Devil. His enthusiasm for his topic had bounded along so vigorously he had far exceeded the limits of good taste. Still, his points contained a kernel of instruction even if they were unnecessarily vituperative. He claimed that young warriors would make love pacts with the widows for a night—wholesale perversion, he called it. Did Navajos observe the same custom? Here was a nubile young widow and a young man who could easily be classed as a warrior had there been any wars at the moment.

Ah, but Linc had fought in a war, albeit a tiny one, with Joe Dasanie. He was not only a warrior, but a winning one. And that poor Doli must be incredibly lonely out here, miles from the nearest person, with only a small boy for company. No wonder Kee was so important to her.

Naomi practically slapped her own face. Shame on her! Here she was groping for excuses to condone immorality, and there was no excuse for immorality. Living in this savage wilderness was warping her better instincts. She really must hie herself back to civilization, and the sooner the better!

She thought briefly of walking out to the hay shed, perhaps to catch those two *in flagrante delicto*. No. Nasty and tempting as that thought might be, she needed Linc Rawlins. She could not find John without Linc's help, and John must be warned about his guides' perfidy. It would not do to check up on the irascible and unpredictable Mr. Rawlins and risk incurring his disfavor. Tempting as it was to spy, she must mind her own business in this stuffy old hogan. If they were actually violating God's precepts, she had best not even know about it. She pulled a chair over to the stove and sat.

Anxious to get started this morning, she had been perfunctory in her prayers. Here was a good time to catch up. If she was indeed straying from the straight path of knowing right and condemning wrong, prayer was the way back to it. She must remember John's safety especially, for peril dogged his steps. She would ask God's help in getting her back on the road quickly, lest Linc become involved with this woman and dally here. She asked a special blessing on little Kee, an innocent victim of circumstance. And she must ask His blessing on the lonely, hapless Doli. In all honesty she realized she certainly didn't want to. Doli was discourteous to the extreme. But then, lack of manners was no measure of a person's qualifications for blessing, and it was the Christian thing to do. She wished her Bible were not in Flagstaff.

Why did asking God to bless an Indian woman weigh so onerously? Prayers for the heathen were part of every active Christian's faith, although such prayers were generally couched in very general terms and not directed toward a single particular heathen. Everything that happened since that feckless stagecoach driver left her behind churned together in her mind. She could not think about any one thing without all the others intruding upon the thought and spoiling it. She closed her eyes and made supplication to God concerning the matters she had just sorted out. She thanked Him for His providence thus far, for providence it was. Now, as she looked at all these confusing events in retrospect, she could see God's protective hand, even if He had not been particularly obvious about demonstrating His love. She gave Him the praise and thanks due a faithful provider.

She opened her eyes eventually and sat quietly in the

encompassing gloom. Linc got along well with this widow woman and they were the right ages. Maybe, when he had delivered Naomi back to John's camp, he would return here. He would check up on little Kee, hang around awhile—perhaps he would marry Doli.

Logically, it was the best solution all around. Linc would gain through marriage some measure of acceptance with the people of his Indian half. In fact, he could be of great service to the tribe in its interaction with white men because of his intimate knowledge of the white man's world. And he could help children learn to read and write; there were all sorts of helpful things he could do. Linc would have companionship. Though he seemed to be a loner, he probably needed it. Kee would have a father; every boy needs a father. Doli would no longer be lonely . . .

. . . And Naomi would be absolutely miserable. She did not want Linc to marry Doli or anyone else. She did not want Linc to be outside with Doli just now. She did not care who else might relieve Doli of her loneliness, so long as it was not Linc. It took her many minutes to come to grips with the simple yet astonishing fact: she was intensely jealous for that crude, unpolished, boyish, gangling half-of-each man.

Some things in life are past all logical explanation.

CHAPTER 11

THE WASTELAND CALLED "the wilderness" in Scripture and "the Painted Desert" by geographers, stretches in a vast and sweeping arc across the northern Arizona territory. Gaudy stripes and splashes ripple across cliff sides. Muted earth colors give the rounded sand hills a soft, almost fluffy appearance. And if the brightly colored soil were not paint enough, sunsets wash the land in reds and purples; sunrises tint it delicate pink and gold.

The snow had long since disappeared, but the moisture it left behind intensified the earth colors. Sprigs of the first spring grass and annuals carpeted washes in lime-green, and the dark evergreen creosote bushes seemed brighter now.

They had been riding the better part of two days now. Naomi must be fairly well enured (or perhaps forever ruined!); she didn't feel too hideously uncomfortable. She immersed herself in the desertscape's beauty and pondered one of its enigmas. Classical geologists (of which, no doubt, John was one) claimed these multicolored layers were laid down over eons. Creationists (with whom she cast her own lot) attributed the layers to the Great Flood. The question: How could something so lovely and soothing as this beautiful desert trigger controversy when ugly things escaped all notice?

But then, who would guess that staid and respected scholars would squabble like children over the privilege of naming the bones of animals long dead? Yet here were Cope and Marsh, and therefore John, and now Naomi and even Linc, all tangled up right in the middle of the imbroglio.

Frankly, Naomi had scant interest in geology and almost none in old bones. She saw no crushing need to hasten in naming animals who certainly could not possibly care whether they were named or not, let alone what the name might be. But John was so unflaggingly exuberant about all this she had better develop some genuine interest of her own.

John. John with his geologist's hammer and fancy black camera, scrambling and climbing and grubbing about in the dirt—was he still well? When Naomi was with Linc and John seemed so far away, she could not manage to drum up much heart-felt concern. Now that they were approaching John, the concern built steadily. It was a curious display of fickleness she would not have guessed of herself. Linc did not seem too worried about John's safety, but then Linc didn't seem to care much for John. Neither did Linc seem to worry about anything at all. All too fatalistically, he permitted life to glide right past him.

"We're there!" Naomi stood up in the stirrups the better to see the broad, lazy wash in the far distance. "I didn't realize we were anywhere near. There is John's camp right out there."

The huddled cluster of tents still perched on their same gentle hill, just as she had first seen them. She looked at them now, though, from a different angle—from a mesa top

97

instead of from below. The little curl of smoke still wandered skyward. The smoke made her feel good. Perhaps things were rolling along on an even keel. Perhaps her fears were, so far, unfounded.

Linc led the way down a steep gully. They rode down a narrow canyon with nearly vertical scarps on either side, then crossed a wide bulge of gravel at the canyon's mouth and wound among boulders higher than the horses' backs. Naomi noticed that the prickly pear pads were fat and smooth from all the spring rain.

The two popped out of the low sand hills and started up the wash which snaked past John's camp. Naomi recognized everything around this area now. Here was a strange and desolate region to feel at home in; yet she did. And if she felt some familiarity with this area, surely Linc must.

"Linc, you must know every square yard of this country."

"Been through most of it."

Why did the answer irritate her? "Been through," she retorted. "Always 'been through.' You're spending the winter in someone else's hogan—no, probably a *hokee-gan*—and you've 'been through' just about every area in two territories. Can't you call anyplace home? How about Kansas? I think you said you lived there till you were nine."

"Always Rawlins' little half-breed kid. Was never really accepted around there."

"Your mother's home then. She grew up where?"

"Bita Hochee and the buttes. Lived a couple years at Chinle. That was her, not me."

"And she met your father there? At Chinle?"

"More or less."

"Getting a complete answer out of you is like plucking a turkey. You just never get it all."

He snorted, a sort of cheerful chuckle. "You want a

complete answer. All right, the army was sent out to stomp on the Dineh because the settlers claimed they were making trouble. The soldiers spent most of their time and attention on Chinle Wash.''

"A big battle.''

"Nope. Slow starvation. The army rode through, ripping up crops and shooting livestock. Eventually the Dineh got hungry enough to knuckle under. Took the army months, though. Pa claimed there was seven thousand and Ma says eight. Anyway, the army managed to round up most of them and walk them east to Fort Sumner in New Mexico.''

"A reservation.''

"An outdoor prison. Army intended to make farmers out of 'em.''

"But you just said the army took months to destroy all their crops and animals.''

"You're catching on. Pa met Ma and courted her more or less on the sly during the march. He snuck her out and married her near Albuquerque. It earned him a dishonorable discharge, but he didn't care. He was fed up with the army anyway. Then he took her to Kansas. Bought a little place down on the Arkansas.''

"It's a very romantic story, really.''

"Yeah, I guess to a woman it might be.''

"And you can't find any clue at all to your mother's whereabouts.''

"Spent two years on it. About ready to give up. I've tried all the places there are to try and a couple more, including her clan and her father's clan.''

"So now you just drift with no purpose whatsoever.''

The sheepskin coat heaved as he shrugged. "We'll see.''

There were the tents right there. Naomi saw no horses at all; John must be gone. Or, Neeskah and perhaps Dasanie had stolen them along with . . . she didn't want to think about it. She kicked her horse's ribs and very nearly entered the camp ahead of Linc.

Linc pivoted Nizhoni near the table, "John? John Carter! Neeskah! *¡Señora* Felicidad!"

Naomi had mentioned Felicidad's name only once, and then casually in passing. Yet he had remembered. Linc was possessed of an enviable gift, the ability to remember names. Naomi lacked it.

Felicidad appeared at the cooktent flap. She wiped fidgety hands on her apron. *"Señorita Morrison. Bienvenido.* Welcome." Her voice trembled. Was she fear-stricken, worried, or simply uncomfortable in the presence of this towering stranger?

Naomi might be hardened to long horseback riding, but she was nonetheless very happy to be able to slide off to the ground. *"Señora, uh, dejame a presentarle a usted el señor Linc Rawlins. Ah, es un amigo, ah . . ."* She had picked up some Spanish in Santa Fe partly in self-defense, for most of her pupils spoke Spanish by preference. Now her bilingualism fled, just when she needed it most. She had no idea if the words were correct or not. She switched to English. *"Señora,* I wish to present Mr. Linc Rawlins, a friend."

Linc seemed not the least interested in correct formal introductions. He hopped off Nizhoni and loomed over the little Spanish lady. "We have to find John Carter. Do you know where he is? Which way he went? *¿Donde 'stá'l señor?"*

She waved her hands vaguely this way and that. "Here, there, dunno. *No se."* She was not just nervous, she was frightened. Naomi felt sorry for her.

"Neeskah. He with Mr. Carter?"

"Uh, theenk so. Don' know."

Naomi brandished her horse's reins. "This is Joe

100

Dasanie's horse. Do you remember? I left on him. Is he here?"

"Joe Dasanie. Ehhh." Her hands were vibrating now.

Impulsively Naomi grabbed the trembling hands into her own. The hands were calloused and cool, all knobby joints and leathern skin. Felicidad worked hard with her hands.

Linc was scowling."He's here? *¿Stá ' qui ' l Dasanie?*"

She glanced up at him briefly and looked elsewhere. "Here, gone again. Somewhere. Don' know."

Linc grabbed two folding stools and plunked them down beside her. He sat on one and motioned toward the other. *"Sientese, señora, por favor. Bueno. Ahora dígame, ¿que pasó aqui esta mañana?"* He rattled it out. If Naomi had wondered about his fluency in Spanish, she wondered no longer.

Naomi's Spanish, though not fluent, had gotten her through some strange conversations in Santa Fe. It was useless now. She could not so much as follow the general drift. Linc asked Felicidad to sit down and tell him what had happened so far that day. Well, she thought that was it. Everything beyond that point was gibberish, a rushing torrent of unintelligible syllables.

The woman stuttered and repeated herself. Naomi remembered some of the place names drawn out of her by Linc's prodding. Ward Terrace. Triassic. She knew from John's bubbling discourses that Triassic deposits were exceedingly common and the terrace extended for scores of miles. It was much too large a haystack to find needles in.

Linc asked his thousand-and-first question.

Felicidad nodded firmly. *"Sí, señor. Una mapa."*

"Hah!" Linc tilted his head. "You're sure he took one. Just one map?"

"One." The lady held up one finger.

101

"Good." Linc hopped up and dashed over to the small table full of maps. "One of these?"

"Jus' one." Felicidad followed him over, waddling rapidly.

Naomi dragged her horse along, not knowing what else to do with it. "John took one of his maps along?"

"Right."

"Then we don't know where he is," she shrugged, "because he has the map telling where he is. I don't get it."

Linc started riffling through the messy pile. "You know that the territory—everywhere, even Ohio—is divided up into parts that are also divided into smaller and smaller parts."

"A section is a square mile and little maps are plats."

"That's the idea. And they're labeled here by latitude and longitude. By coordinates. We sort them out by coordinates and see which map's missing. That'll probably be the map John took with him—the most likely place to look for him. A few minutes spent now should save us hours trying to track them."

"Not 'us.' 'You.' I couldn't track a dog with muddy paws."

"Help me." He plopped half the ungainly pile on Naomi's arm. In desperation she sat down on the ground and let them sag into her lap. He tapped the top one. "Lower corner there, see?"

"I see. I lost track of your conversation right after you asked Felicidad to sit down. Then what?"

"Here's 36-10. Prob'ly too far south."

"You didn't answer my question. What happened this morning? Here's 35-50."

He was juggling his sheaf awkwardly. It was the first time Naomi had ever seen him do anything awkwardly. He shifted the whole pile and started over. "John left camp about the usual time. Neeskah was with him taking care of

102

the pack mule. Almost noon, Dasanie walked into the camp with his arm in a sling.''

"Good. That relieves you of the onus of being responsible for a man's death. So he's hale and hearty.''

"It's a mixed blessing. He flashed his knife around a little, gave Felicidad a hard time trying to get her to tell him where John and Neeskah went. She didn't remember. She truly didn't remember even which way they left camp, and he thought for awhile she was lying. Really had her scared. Finally he walked about a quarter mile out and started working a circle.''

"What do you mean?" These maps were in no semblance of order. Naomi wondered how John could find anything. Most of them were well penciled.

"He walked in a wide circle around the camp looking for the freshest tracks out, so he could follow them.''

"Isn't that time-consuming? Why didn't he simply wait until this evening when they'll come back in?"

"Thirty-six-40. Probably too far north. Dasanie has no way of knowing whether we've reached John yet or not. He can't afford to take the chance that John is wise to their plans and maybe is lying in wait for him right now. He'll want to sneak in, talk to Neeskah alone.''

That now-familiar cold chill zigged down her back again.

Linc flipped rapidly through his map corners. "Where's 36-aught by 111-30?"

Naomi shuffled again through her share. "I don't have it.''

"You sure?"

"Yes, I'm sure. These are all 35's—except this one.''

Linc pointed northeast. "Then that's where he is, right at the base of that scarp, where it extends out to a point. Here's the map next east of John's, and there's where that wash comes down off the mesa. See?"

She compared the map with the distant cliff. "Sort of," she mumbled.

Linc plopped his pile back on the table and jogged over to Nizhoni. He scooped up his reins and swirled aboard in one quick movement. "You wait here, Naomi." Nizhoni pivoted and lunged, and they clattered away.

"Oh, no you don't!" Naomi left the maps lying on the ground. She jumped up and managed to throw the looped reins over her horse's ears on the third attempt. She physically connected Felicidad's hand to her horse's bridle. "Hold this beast!" She poked her toe in a stirrup. "That man isn't leaving me behind!" She clambered up into the saddle. She was getting rather good at this feat, if she did say so herself.

Befuddled, Felicidad simply let go. Naomi gathered up the reins and slammed her heels in the pony's ribs. How glad she was that riding a horse recklessly and full-tilt was actually less bumpy than trying to negotiate a more leisurely pace.

Her horse seemed to understand that it ought to follow after Nizhoni, but it took a rather dim view of moving swiftly. Impatient with its cavalier attitude, she swatted its shoulders with the romal, the rein ends. Improvement followed immediately. There in the distance went Linc. Still, not until Linc pulled up on a small copse to rest Nizhoni did she catch up.

He scowled as she rode up beside him. Her own horse was blowing noisily and sweating. Lather foamed on its neck.

She smiled sweetly. "You said I was an adult capable of making my own decisions, remember? Very well. I just decided to follow you."

"If brains were gold, you'd have to float a loan to buy a newspaper. Dasanie and Neeskah are together by now, comparing notes. If they happen to see you, they'll catch you. Think of all the fine deals they can make with a valuable hostage like you."

"You forget I have Dasanie's horse. He can't catch me."

"And you forget Neeska still has his own horse. They'll catch you. Now listen to me and go back with Felicidad."

Sometimes the best counter to an argument is none at all. She changed the subject. "Have you seen them?"

He sighed, defeated, and nodded. "Recognize your bonedigger up there?"

"Where?"

His long arm pointed. "That little black pimple out on the *bahada*."

"What is a *bahada*? And I think referring to him as a pimple indicates a bad attitude. That black spot? It doesn't even look like a person."

"It looks like a camera on legs with a big black cloth draped over it. He's up under the curtain taking pictures. And a *bahada* is the slope around the base of mountains and cliffs."

"I see. And have you seen the two guides yet?"

"They should be around close. That's what worries me. Neeskah will have told Dasanie by now that we haven't been back yet. So they'll probably consider jumping John before we show up. Now will you please go back to . . . no. I don't want you wandering all over the map alone. Stay with me. Stay right behind me." He barely tightened his legs. Nizhoni lurched forward and loped down off the knoll. Naomi kicked her horse and he obediently fell in behind.

Where was Linc going? She had no idea. He started Nizhoni up a little mound of dirty gray sand, then reined in suddenly and raised his arm. Naomi recognized it as the universal wagonmaster's signal to stop. She stopped. She looked all around. Nothing. She listened carefully. Silence.

An evening breeze was beginning to riffle the dead calm of late afternoon. She turned in the saddle. She could see John clearly from here, silhouetted against the glowing sky. Apparently he had completed his photography. He was out from under the black curtain and dismantling his camera set-up.

"Go tell John to keep his head down! Hurry!" Linc's voice carried a strident edge of urgency, quite unlike him. He plunged Nizhoni off across the hillside toward a steep little draw.

It was time to obey unquestioningly, but Naomi had considerable trouble convincing her horse it was no longer to follow after Linc. When she swatted the horse again with the romal, he danced in a wide circle, stubborn and confused. Stupid animal!

Then she saw them. They were far up that steep draw, both of them. Dasanie's white sling stood out smartly against the dull shadows of the hill. Linc was now somewhere between her and them, but she could not see him; he was behind some bit of rolling desert waste.

Dasanie was standing by a boulder watching in the general direction of that distant bahada—watching John. Neeskah balanced an ungainly pistol across the top of the boulder, cradling it in two hands. Quite plainly, Linc would not reach them in time. And how would he stop them if he did? They had the gun! Naomi could surely never reach John in time to warn him.

Neeskah bent low behind his sights, taking careful aim. And the target in his sights was John Harrison Carter.

106

CHAPTER 12

SUDDENLY NAOMI REMEMBERED the pall of utter helpless-
ness that had choked her when, as a six-year-old, she had
watched her baby sister die of pneumonia. That same pall
shrouded her now. How far did that particular pistol fire a
bullet accurately? Probably Linc knew; certainly John did.
Naomi did not, except to assume it would reach John accurately enough. She must break Neeskah's concentration
immediately and, if possible, draw his fire. She shrieked, a
howl that would make a hyena envious, the only long-
distance weapon in a woman's arsenal.

The two men moved as a cloud of blue gunsmoke lifted
away from Neeskah's hands. She had cried out too late! She
looked back toward the ridge as the black camera toppled.
John dropped from sight. John! The only thing that mattered
was John.

She urged her horse across a low hillside and up the steep
and crumbling slope toward John's erstwhile camera spot.
The loose stones clattered. She leaned forward against the
horse's neck and clung to the saddle horn; still every stride

convinced her she would slide right off the back. They topped out so suddenly she almost rode right past John's crumpled body. She hauled the clumsy bay horse in and turned around. In the arroyo far below, that gun blasted again. Its echo boomed from behind, from beside, from behind again. She slid out of the saddle. She must not let the horse get away. She pulled the reins over its head and hung onto the loop. The nervous bay danced wide, dusty arcs around her.

John moaned. She could not discern the wail, but she could certainly hear its despair.

She dropped down beside him. "Where? Where are you hurt?"

He stared at her incredulously. "I thought you were in Flag! Why did he bring you back?"

"I'll explain later. Linc is here. You know, the man who brought me in the other time. He's very good with gunshot wounds. There was this little boy, and he . . . John? Where are you bleeding?"

"Bleeding? Who, me? I'm not . . . I didn't . . . I don't understand what's going on here at all."

"If you aren't hurt, why did you fall down?"

Below them that gun fired again. And here they sat right out in the open, as exposed as crows on a fencepost. Neeskah must be a terrible shot . . . or else he was shooting not at them but at Linc!

"Here!" She splacked the romal into John's hand. She was done fighting that obstinate nag. She could do better afoot. She ran, leaping and flying, down the steep hillside. The loose and ragged dirt gave way beneath her feet. She had last seen the villainous twosome over beyond those rocks. That was as good a destination as any; if the guides were there, Linc would be near.

Within a few moments she appreciated the value of a

horse in this wasted country. She was out of her first breath and could not yet catch her second. Her lungs burned. She gulped air, but the fire would not go out. She paused on one of those rippling little hills. You would think she could see all around from this little hilltop, but all she could see were higher little hills, and the looming scarp above them.

Beyond the rise to the east, a horse was coming. She listened. No, the horse seemed to be headed away from her, probably angling more to the south. The rider popped out from behind one hill and disappeared instantly behind another. She waited, watching. There he went, nearly a half mile away and quartering to the south, riding hard. He leaned low against his roan's ewed neck and lashed it with the romal.

Another horse was headed in the same direction now in hot pursuit. That must be Linc. But why would he pursue a fleeing Neeskah when John's protection and hers ought logically to come first? And where was Joe Dasanie in all this?

Yes, there went Nizhoni out beyond that final little hill, racing at full speed. What a lovely horse he was with his neck stretched out and his tail cocked high! He would catch up with Neeskah's roan shortly.

But Joe Dasanie was riding him!

Her heart thudded. There was only one way Joe Dasanie could have gotten his larcenous hands on Nizhoni. Where was Linc? What had they done to him? Her legs must function without help from her lungs if need be; she was pampering her body when she ought to be running. Stumbling forward, she jogged out across the rolling desert. She tried to hurry, but her legs and lungs refused to be rushed. The fastest she could muster was a frantic sort of walk.

Once upon a time, when she was young and life was simple, she had run down a hill so fast she could not stop even though she winded herself. She was paying for that now; her lungs had never forgiven her indiscretion. Now she could run only a short distance before they began to ache and fill with fluid. She was gasping and coughing, sounding like a candidate for the paupers' infirmary.

Linc was so fairly covered with dust and dirt she didn't see him until he moved. How could she have run such a distance and still be so far away? He was on his side. He rolled to his hands and knees groggily. His head drooped low. He moved slowly, drawing his legs up to sit tricornered, his elbows draped across his knees and his head bowed forward against his arms. He looked ghastly.

Apparently he heard her coming. He raised his head to look at her. She crumpled into a weary pile at his side, still so winded she could not speak immediately. "Are you . . . ? I saw Nizhoni. I'm so sorry."

He stared at her numbly. "Dasanie took Nizhoni."

She nodded, feeling almost as miserable as he looked. Little cords of fresh blood wandered down the side of his head, detoured around his ear, and soaked into his collar. She would cry, but she was too exhausted. She fumbled for her hankie. What do you say to a man who has just lost his beloved horse mostly because of you?

He picked up a pebble and dashed it down again. He gazed off to the south. The boy-child in him showed through; he looked so hurt, so vulnerable. Lost for words, she handed him her hankie and let him dab at his own head.

He looked at her. "You were supposed to get yourself up to the bone-digger and stay there. Is he dead?"

"I don't think he's hurt at all. I mean, he doesn't think so. He has my horse. I left it there. I was afraid for you. The gun . . . I didn't know what to do." She sighed, more a sob than anything else. "Then when I saw Nizhoni . . . Linc, every time I think things are terrible, they get worse. I don't know how to help or what to do. Except pray."

"Yeah. Pray." His head plopped forward on his arms again.

"You look so . . . so . . . disconsolate. What can I do? I feel responsible, in a way. If it weren't for me, none of this would have happened to you."

He took a deep breath and sat up straight. He was looking off to the south again. "They won't go far. I'll get him back."

"You don't think they'll just go away forever?"

"We're sitting ducks. Unarmed, perched out on that point. And they're mad now, Dasanie especially. He has a score to settle. It isn't just a matter of robbing an easy dude."

"I'd hardly call John an easy dude to rob."

"Musta left his brains behind at Yale when he hired those two," Linc groaned as he twisted around to his knees and lurched to his feet. She stood beside him, half expecting to have to prop him up. He gazed wearily at John's ridge. "Let's head up that way. Don't think I'm gonna climb that hill. Get our heads together. Plan some kind of battle strategy. And move that camp."

"I doubt John will be much inclined to move until the last of his maps are penciled in. He had some blank ones in the pile yet." She fell in beside him as he started walking. "Besides, couldn't they follow us even if we moved? Track us?"

"Move in closer to civilization. Closer to Moenkopi or down nearer Flag. We're in the middle of nowhere here; too far to go for help if we need it. The farmers and ranchers around here keep peace vigilante-style, but they keep it."

"But what if John isn't quite done here?"

"He's done." Linc stopped. He stood a few minutes,

breathing quietly, before continuing across the crunchy gravel.

They did not have to attempt to climb that steep slope. John came riding down it on his sorrel. He led the mule off one side and Naomi's horse off the other. The mule was loaded haphazardly, with camera legs and pieces sticking out of the pannier. John rode in beside them and swung his sorrel around. He was a magnificent horseman.

Linc took the bay's reins without being asked. He stuffed a moccasined foot into the stirrup and dragged himself into the saddle. It was the first time Naomi had ever seen him use stirrups to mount.

John cleared his throat. "The horse is intended for Miss Morrison."

Naomi stepped up to John's knee. "It's quite all right, John. Really."

"What was all that anyway? Who was shooting at me?" He was asking her, not Linc, John's hazel eyes on hers.

"Your two guides. Neeskah pulled the trigger, but Dasanie is in it quite as heavily."

"Your instincts were right." He wagged his head. "I didn't even know he owned a gun."

Linc drew a deep breath. "He didn't, until he lifted the Paterson out of your tent this noon. Felicidad told me."

"My own gun?!" John sounded incredulous, and greatly disappointed. He looked down at Naomi. "Then if Dasanie was . . . did he hurt you?"

"No, though he intended to. Linc here interceded."

"Oh, he did." John looked suspicious, not grateful.

Linc vacated a stirrup. Naomi tucked her foot into it and hauled herself up. This time Linc did nothing to help her. She got there on her own and felt rather proud perched behind him. She was getting much better at this horsemanship business, even if it were not ladylike.

She looked down into the pannier on the mule. "John, your camera is in there all ajumble. Won't it be damaged, bouncing around like that?"

John looked at her with eyes as woebegone as Linc's. "There are approximately one hundred fourteen thousand square miles comprising the territory of Arizona, including Indian reserves. At six hundred and forty acres to the square mile, that's, about seventy-three million acres. Each acre contains roughly forty-eight hundred square yards, not including vertical variation. That's perhaps three hundred and fifty thousand million square yards altogether."

He studied her dolefully, as a child who had just lost a puppy might appeal to his mother. "Of all those three hundred and fifty thousand million square yards in the territory of Arizona where they might have sent a bullet, they had to fire one straight into the single square yard in all the territory which held my beautiful camera."

CHAPTER 13

THERE IS A PIVOTAL moment in the desert evening, a single breath, when day becomes night. The air shifts abruptly from warm to cool and you can feel the shift. Daylight lingers, clings to the purple peaks, clutches at whatever wispy clouds may hang near the horizon, then flees in its final instant. But most telling of all, the vastness—the sheer expanse—suddenly and unexpectedly shrinks down to nearness. Even under a rising moon the once-distant desert collapses to a close intimacy of grays and blacks.

Naomi sat on a folding stool and leaned back against the cooktent center pole. The clear, cold desert night came tiptoeing in to linger behind her shoulders, to huddle just outside the ring of sallow lamplight. She felt uncomfortable engulfed thusly in the ocean of darkness. She wished it were later in the year, when darkness did not come so quickly.

She finished the last of her tea and cradled the cup and saucer in her lap. Felicidad came by presently, taking Naomi's cup and saucer and scooping John's off the table, before John had quite finished his tea. However, he made no notice. He was too busy poking forlornly at the dead hulk of his camera.

The horses were tethered here within the circle of tents, lest Neeskah and Dasanie make themselves richer by another horse or two. In the dimness beyond the table, the blaze face of John's sorrel horse bobbed.

The coal oil lamp on the table flickered. John reached out absently and adjusted the wick. His folding stool creaked as he shifted his weight.

Leaving the remnants of his ravaged camera on the table, John stood up to stretch. "Irreparable. From splendid instrument to sorry little heap in a single moment. There's no justice."

"I appreciate that your camera is the finest of its kind—*was* the finest, I might say—but that bullet rattling around inside it could well be rattling around inside you right now. God spared you miraculously, yet you complain."

He snickered condescendingly. "Ah, the eternal optimism of womankind. Always the silver lining. I agree I'm lucky, after a fashion. But I would heal, and this instrument won't. Frankly I would almost rather it had been me; not fatally, of course."

"Why that's bordering on blasphemy, John Carter! To imply that our Lord erred in such an important matter."

A shrill, warbling whistle echoed off the rocks east of camp. Naomi sat up straight.

John scowled. "Is that supposed to be a signal? I don't remember arranging anything with your Rawlins fellow."

Naomi shook her head. "I don't know what it would mean. Perhaps he needs help. But surely he'd call out, not whistle." Somehow she felt assured that the whistle was indeed Linc's, and not the two guides signaling each other, but she could not say why she felt so. It was a feeling and

115

that was all. She would not mention it to John. If he sneered at her optimism, what must he think of womanly intuition?

They listened to the hovering darkness. Long minutes later the whistle trilled again, southwest of the camp.

"Where is Rawlins, anyway?" John paced from tent to tent, listening. Was it a rhetorical question or a question directed at her? She would answer it anyway.

"He said he'd be watching out there awhile. I'm not sure precisely how he intended to go about it. He thinks those two will sneak in on us, and I believe him. You know, we do stand out rather like sore thumbs. Sitting ducks, if you will."

John paused beside her in his perambulations. "I'm not as quick to trust him as you seem to be. He could well be one of them."

"How can you say such a thing? He and Dasanie were bent on killing each other. It was no dramatization, I assure you."

"And just how did he manage to show up at the crucial moment if they aren't in this together?"

"He told me he was . . ."

"Shh!" John held up a finger. He cocked an ear toward the darkness. "Someone out there, I believe." He squinted into the blackness, his eyes darting. He snatched up a folding stool and snapped it shut. Thus armed, he trod silently to the edge of the far tent.

Naomi listened intently, but heard nothing at all.

"The water still hot?" Linc's voice sent her a foot straight up, weary as she was. He stood at the edge of the cooktent.

John wheeled. "Where did you . . . ? I heard something off that way a moment ago." He pointed.

"Prob'ly me." Linc leaned heavily against the cooktent end pole.

116

"Why did you whistle?" Naomi trusted her instincts, even if John would not.

"That was Nizhoni's 'come here' whistle. If he was anywhere in earshot, he would have ripped up stakes and come to me, or at least raised a big ruckus trying. He's nowhere around. That means Dasanie and Neeskah are gone too. All the same, we better keep a watch going tonight."

Felicidad stuck her head out of the cooktent flap. "Coffee or tea, *señor* Rawlins?"

"Coffee if you have it, thank you."

She nodded. "Five minutes, new pot. *Sí, señor!*" The head disappeared and a second later popped back out. "Sugar?"

"Gracias, no."

Felicidad went back inside. Naomi noticed she was grinning cheerfully.

Naomi stood up and stretched. Oh, but she ached, though not as much as she would have a week ago. She was getting tougher. "Gentlemen, I expect to do my full share of standing watch or pounding upon miscreants with folding stools or whatever defensive action must be taken. Please awaken me when it's my turn at watch. Good night, Mr. Carter. Good night, Mr. Rawlins."

John tipped toward her in a cavalier bow. Linc barely nodded. She slipped through the cooktent flap from pallid lamp light into dimmer candle light. At the back of the tent Felicidad fiddled with the coffeepot on the little iron stove. Naomi wished coffee tasted as good as it smelled.

"Buenas noches, Felicidad."

"Buenas noches, señorita."

Naomi wriggled down into her bedroll without removing her shoes. Should some emergency arise, she must be ready to run. Besides, it was cold tonight. She heard John's stool creak as he sat down again. By chance her cot was in the

117

corner of the cooktent nearest the table outside, and her head was nearly against the canvas.

Linc's lanky shadow poured across the glowing canvas. He crossed to the stool she had vacated and carried it to the table. He plopped down there between the lamp and the cooktent; his shadow loomed against the canvas by her head. He leaned forward both elbows on the table. No doubt he suffered a thundering headache.

The men were silent for several minutes. Naomi saw no shadow from John—he was beyond the lamp—but his stool creaked with every shift and movement. She pictured him staring pensively at his defunct camera. Poor John. They mumbled together, general things about moving the camp or not moving the camp. Naomi thought she heard her name mentioned. She drifted toward sleep.

The voices were now just barely audible through the dense canvas.

John: ". . . to worry if you didn't see any sign of them out there."

Linc: "I circled the camp twice, slow, but that doesn't mean much. I imagine they would've jumped me if they'd known I was there, but they may not have been looking for us out in the dark. You can bet they aren't gone for good even if they left for the night."

John: "Oh, I don't know. So far they've been bested every step of the way. Surely they'll give up soon."

Linc: "Gonna tell the sheriff when you reach civilization again? Maybe the army?"

John: "Absolutely. They were shooting at me with my own stolen gun." He sounded a bit impatient.

Linc: "Right. And you think they're gonna just back off and let you do that. You make a formal complaint, give everyone in the territory a complete description of them, and they're gonna politely wait until you get around to it."

John: "You're saying they'd kill us just to shut us up. They wouldn't dare try."

Linc: "They already tried, Carter. Wake up."

John: "You're overstating the danger."

Linc: "If anything, I'm understating it. You wanna risk your neck chasing dead dinosaurs, fine. But don't risk Naomi's. Let's get her down to Flagstaff tomorrow. Both of us, first light, as fast as we can travel."

John: "First-name basis with her, are you? Interesting. Tell me, just when did you come upon her in that so-called fracas with Dasanie? And how long has she been in your company?"

The shadow shoulders heaved in a mighty shrug. "If that were any business of yours, which it isn't, I'd take the trouble to piece this last week together exactly. But I don't feel like catering to your idle curiosity. She's innocent and you know it and by the grace of God she'll stay that way till she chooses different. Was that Paterson the only gun around? How about Felicidad? She bring along a pocket piece maybe?"

John was beginning to sound testy. The day was wearing thin on everybody. "No she didn't. I asked. Actually, those two aren't that deeply into trouble yet. They stole only the gun."

"And my horse."

"Which can be traded, presumably, for their horse. Maybe we can strike a deal with them. It's worth the try." His voice fell. "Except for the camera, it's ruined."

Linc grunted. "Naomi said how proud of it you were. Twenty-fifth of a second, huh? No hope for resurrection?"

"No miracles in the offing. I'll take the corpse back to New Haven. I suppose our equipment supplier can salvage parts. Lenses seem intact, and the shutter mechanism. You and Miss Morrison must have had some extraordinarily

119

lengthy conversations, if my humble camera has been a topic."

Linc snorted. "Nothing you own or do is humble, Carter. She's smart. Carries a conversation well. Listens."

John's stool creaked. "I'm a firm believer in place, Rawlins."

"Which means?"

"You and Miss Morrison do not occupy the same place."

The shadow nodded slowly. "Yep. No two objects can occupy the same place at the same time. Archimedes figured that one out a couple thousand years ago."

Naomi almost giggled aloud. She recognized the playful overtone in Linc's voice. He was matching wits with John, just as he often toyed with her. She admired all over again his marvelous memory. She had mentioned John's camera only once, as she described John on the ride up here this morning. And he had remembered.

Oblivious to the banter outside, Felicidad was putting the final touches to her serving tray. Besides coffee for Linc, there was a pot of tea for John, the honey jar, and biscuits left over from supper. She assumed, probably correctly, that they would be up for some time yet. She hummed to herself, a charming little tune, and carefully squeezed and patted her hair into place. She glanced self-consciously toward Naomi as she started toward the flap with her tray.

Naomi whispered, *"Muy guapo, ¿eh, Felicidad?"* which she hoped meant that Linc was very handsome.

Felicidad glowed and giggled softly. *Guapo, sí, y cortes. Tan cortes. Un caballero verdadero."* Radiant as the rising sun, Felicidad swept out the tentflap.

Naomi smiled. She knew *caballero*. Gentleman. Felicidad thought that crude, brusque, rough-hewn man was a gentleman. And yet, the Spanish culture was rich in elegance. A Spanish gentleman was a gentleman indeed. The *cortes* took her a moment to decipher. *Cortesía.* Courtesy. Felicidad also thought Linc was courteous. Well, that said how much Felicidad knew about men. But then, Naomi could not fault him for his gentle thoughtfulness during the snowstorms, when all the world collapsed around her ears. He was a courteous gentleman in the foundational sense, the truest sense. He was gentle and thoroughly trustworthy.

John: "That'll be all tonight, Felicidad."

Linc: "*Qué considerada. Muchas gracias, señora.*"

"*De nada, Señor Rawlins. Buenas noches.*"

"*Buenas noches.*" The way Link and Felicidad pronounced the phrase and the way it came from Naomi's lips differed radically. She must brush up on her Spanish pronunciation.

Felicidad came back in. She bobbed her head; her point was proven, obviously. "*¿Eh? Cortes.*" She blew out the candle and shuffled about at her cot. The tent canvas glowed brighter now that the interior light was out. Naomi turned her attention to the conversation outside. It was louder now, and plain to make out. Did she detect an undercurrent of hostility? It seemed so.

John was speaking and she regretted instantly that she had not heard the preceding. "I find this whole exchange fascinating. I detect that you despise me, am I right? But you're being very subtle about it. I'll give you that. So let's be open, Rawlins. Exactly what is the source of your animosity towards me? Jealousy?"

Linc was silent a moment. The shadow moved as he wagged his head. "Naw. Jealous of what? No, I guess it's just bad comparisons. Your attitude reminds me of a fellow named Tom Oakes."

"Don't believe I've heard of him."

"Prob'ly not. When my father died, Ma decided to move back to New Mexico. But when she got to Bosque Redondo, the Dineh had long since left. No Navajos at all left at Fort Sumner. So she came over to Arizona territory looking for her clan. Searched around the buttes, Chinle, Bita Hochee. No one. She ended up marrying a white man, a trader, because she had to do something.''

"Tom Oakes."

"Tom Oakes. She wasn't his wife—she was his slave. He had the same attitude exactly toward women that you do. Any women. You got your dog and your gun and your horse and your wife. Maybe reverse the order on the dog and the horse.'' The shadow picked up a biscuit. "That's why you irritate me, I suppose. Tom Oakes. Except you'd stick bones and cameras somewhere up front there with the dog.''

"Interesting viewpoint. Pity you don't really grasp the pyramidal structure of modern society as it really is.''

"I grasp that Naomi Morrison knows what she wants and she has the spine to try and get it. I admire her for that. And when she matches up some day, I'll bet you she doesn't meekly step in line behind any dog or horse—or camera.''

"There's much more to admire in Naomi Morrison than you have the capacity to see, Rawlins.''

Naomi's breastbone tickled. That was Phoebus speaking admiringly in her behalf!

"She appreciates the finer things of life, the niceties of our culture,'' John continued. "In fact, her love of knowledge and her quick mind equip her to be the perfect wife of a college professor. She's sensible. Able to handle simple duties well. Pretty—a nice plus if you want to impress the higher-ups. Her nose isn't going to peel forever. I'm considering taking her back to New Haven with me.''

"You sound like she has about as much choice in the matter as a horse at a farm auction. Up for grabs.''

"Choice? You seem to think selecting a life consort is like selecting apples at the greengrocer's. There's a decorum—a custom—of which you are obviously unaware. We'd stop in Ohio along the way, or wherever it is she's from. I'd meet her family and ask her father for her hand. She may be on her own, but it's the proper thing so long as her father's still alive. And if we married before traveling east, of course, I'd ask his blessing on the union. Matter of form, you know. Understand, that's all conjectural at this point. I haven't made any decision. Haven't even fully considered it yet. There are some other prospects.''

"That's all very well and good—except she's not going east. She's traveling west to 'Frisco. Alone.''

"That was merely an interim plan on her part.''

"'Merely'!'' The shadow moved. "It's what she wants more than anything else. That—and looking good in front of her God.''

John's voice was creamy-smooth to be so full of acid. "There, you see? You've made my point for me. You can't hope to grasp her finer qualities. The way you said that just now—your tone of voice—made it an afterthought, something tacked on. That's one of her most admirable attributes—her desire to keep up appearances. Very valuable in a wife to keep the appearance of virtue. Good reflection on the husband. And you failed to appreciate it properly. I admit her religious proclivities are unsophisticated. Believing the Bible literally, swallowing the myths could be a drawback in conversation with more enlightened colleagues. But she grew up on a farm as I understand, or at least in rural circumstances of some sort. It's amazing she's as well read as she is. Once she's exposed to a more expanded point of view about religion, she'll come around.''

"Farmers are dumb, and you city boys aren't.''

"Dumb? I certainly wouldn't put it that way. Conservative. Slow to step out beyond tradition.''

Linc's voice was taking on that playful edge again. "She

didn't say this in so many words, understand. But from the way she talks, her father's sure no sharecropper. Wealthy and respected. Four hundred acres of black bottomland in northern Ohio seems to be . . .''

"Oh?" John sounded absolutely suspicious now. "You've been checking on her background? Measuring the size of her purse, maybe."

"I told you we were talking on the way up here yesterday. We both appreciate a good farm, well kept. My Pa's was the best and so's hers."

Naomi smiled in the darkness. He had promised to keep silent about those two harmless but suspicious-looking days, and he was remaining true to his word.

Linc continued, "Anyway, a good farm seems to me to be better credentials to present at the pearly gates than an enlightened attitude towards your modern religion. I bet if God had to choose between a good farmer and a good college professor, he'd pick the farmer every time."

John sniggered. "But of course God chooses according to wealth."

"Nope. Convenience. Don't have to reach near as far, 'cause the farmer's so much closer to Him."

Naomi buried her mouth and nose in both hands to keep from howling with glee. She nearly burst. She must not weigh too heavily the fact that Linc, the pagan, was defending the God of Scripture. He was playing with John, toying with him. He probably had no new respect for God. If John had taken the opposite stance, Linc would have expressed a liberal view just to contradict him. Still, the fact that Linc defended both God and farmers, even if teasingly, delighted her.

The stool creaked. "This is fruitless. Mildly amusing, but worthless. If I decide to take Naomi's hand, it's certainly no business of yours. The matter's ended."

"You'll be surprised what business I make of it. If she thinks she'd like to see 'Frisco, I'm gonna put her on a train for California."

"Ah. Finally we're getting to the core of this meaningless chatter. I assure you, Rawlins, that Miss Morrison entertains expectations far beyond the life of a squaw in some remote hogan. You dishonor her by so much as thinking of courting her."

"Courting her? A man stands up for a woman's right to enjoy the same privileges Indian women do—and he's *courting* her?"

"Please demonstrate just how an Indian squaw fares any better than the woman in the meanest of white families." John's voice dripped acid. Naomi was afraid he had Linc there.

"The Hopi leaders are all men. Know who chooses 'em? Hopi women. The women—and not just Hopis—decide who marries who and whether to divorce. They own their own property and make their own decisions. Are you ready to grant those privileges to your wife?"

John's voice reeked of contempt. "The supreme vanity, Rawlins. You challenge the very foundation of modern civilization—the family structure. When your squaws live in proper houses and use table linen, you may tell me how society should be run."

"First thing Pa bought my Ma when they got to Kansas was a clothes mangle to do up her tablecloths. And one of those Atlantic Queen ranges. He was truly proud of that stove. She even started all her fires with real matches. None of this rubbing two hotheads together to make sparks. That's not civilized."

Naomi sat up. Linc's voice might be flowing oil-smooth, but he was boiling mad. She could feel it.

John was fuming too. "And you are now telling me

what's civilized. Your problem, Rawlins, is that you've been exposed to just enough white culture to suffer delusions of grandeur.''

Naomi's feet were on the floor. She didn't hear Linc's reply over the rustle of her blankets, but the shadow was sitting bolt upright. This silly bickering must stop before it got out of hand, and she was the one to stop it. She marched to the tent flap and slammed outside.

Once John waxed hot on a subject—any subject, be it dinosaurs or Benjamin Harrison's imminent presidency —he hurtled through it like a runaway railroad train. He was wound up now. He had risen slightly off his stool and was wagging a finger in Linc's face. ''And you will not presume to tell me what's best for a woman of refinement and breeding. You may well . . .''

Linc was half off his stool like a cat coiled to pounce when Naomi shouted ''No!'' She cared not a whit that she had just cut John off in mid-sentence. They both snapped around, startled, and stared at her.

''Enough, both of you! Our mutual enemies are those scalawags cowering out there in the darkness, and you will kindly stop pecking at each other like two new hens in the same coop. Good night again, gentlemen.'' She turned away, then turned back again to them. ''Incidentally, gentlemen, if and when I choose to marry, or travel, or do any other thing, it is I who will choose, and not either one of you. Is that understood?'' She stomped back into the tent and flopped violently onto her cot.

The table was silent. Good. Linc's shadow stood up. He mumbled something about taking a turn around. The shadow washed across the canvas and leaped off the far corner.

Felicidad whispered hoarsely, ''¿Que pasó, señorita? ¿Una disputa?''

126

"Yes. Just a silly dispute. It's finished. All over."

"¿Concerniente a usted?"

"What about? Nothing important. Nothing important at all. Good night, Felicidad." She burrowed into her blankets again, in such turmoil she could not lie still, let alone think. The longer she lay there, the angrier she became. John was right. That brazen Indian presumed much too much. And Linc was right also. John too much assumed that he would have whatever he wanted without deference to her own wishes. They were both impossible, absolutely impossible. She could not wait to get to San Francisco.

CHAPTER 14

THE WORST PART of getting out of bed in the morning is always the shock of leaving the nest. No matter how warm the day or how well one is clothed, there is that slap as the world accosts you full-face. A moment ago Naomi's feet had been toasty warm. Despite the fact that she was already clothed and shod, her feet went cold the moment she put them on the ground. Her fingers chilled. The whole morning would no doubt be frigid, for the air was frosty today, even inside the cooktent.

She heard no war or insurrection outside; so the brouhaha between the two belligerents last night was apparently done for good. Those two . . . honestly! She stretched and stepped out into bright morning sun. She smiled, a demonstration of complete forgiveness. "Good morning, John!"

"Good morning!" He stood at the washstand by the other tent, his face half immersed in lather, his razor in his hand. A clean shirt hung in readiness from the tent's end pole. He must take his shirt off when he worked out in the field, because his whole upper torso was sun-bronzed. The muscles in his arms and shoulders flexed and rippled as he angled his razor. Phoebus!

"You slept well, I trust," Naomi smiled more widely.

"Thank you, yes. And you look refreshed this morning."

"Refreshed and frozen must appear similar. When does it get hot in the desert."

"It'll warm up quickly enough. I think we've seen the last of foul weather."

"Lord willing! Linc is still asleep?"

"Our watchdog remained on the alert most of the night."

"And neither of you called me for my turn at the helm. Very well, tonight I shall be watchdog." She lingered a moment, simply watching him move. Then, in a burst of self-discipline, she turned away to leave him in peace with his morning toilet. She walked out beyond the tents a few steps and stopped.

The early sun tinged distant scarps pink and gave the morning haze a rosy hue. The desert colors were especially crisp, the wash especially green. She walked ten feet and sat down on a low boulder. The air was clear but for the ground haze, and her mind was clear. Right now was the time to think. She folded her hands and composed herself a moment, savoring the lovely and gentle desert. Last night seemed remote now, and manageable. Why was it so frustrating at the time?

"Hens in a coop," she had said. She smiled. Her reference to chickens betrayed her farm roots thoroughly. Well, that's what she was—a farm girl. She loved Linc's spirited defense of farmers. He was quite right. Farmers are closer to the earth which, paradoxically, puts them closer to heaven. John was a city man, born removed from the God-made world. He probably didn't know any farmers personally and would not have guessed that her own father was not only well read but a patron of the new art museum in Toledo. Naturally John held a somewhat stilted view of farmers, with none in his inner circle of friends. She remembered Linc talking about farming in Alberta. He would be a very good farmer, the good stewardship of that hogan where he stayed was proof of that. But he'd never actually farmed. Drifters never possessed the initiative to do better for themselves.

She had left the farm, but apparently the farm had not left her. No doubt some of the tears that had erupted uncontrollably last night were simple homesickness. Still, those men must take their share of blame for upsetting her so. Even in the cheerful light of day, she yearned to be in Ohio, to sit in Mama's cozy kitchen; to stand in the bier and listen to the cows grind hay into milk; to pat Bess and Tony the dray horses, all steamy from dragging in the last of the dead trees from the woodlot.

Horses. Poor Linc. He tried to do her a simple favor and his bitter reward was to lose his precious Nizhoni, his beautiful horse. And that was not to mention the damage done his poor head. She couldn't blame him for being a bit testy last night. By rights he should just walk away from this whole mess, try to find Nizhoni, and start over far removed from Naomi and the problems that dogged her so constantly. Her predicament wasn't his responsibility. Maybe he should just go back to Doli.

Doli. The thought of Linc marrying Doli did not bother her so much, now that she had been in John's company again.

John. He certainly fit the image of the perfect mate with which she had furnished her dreams long ago. Phoebus. He was exactly the kind of man she was traveling to San Francisco to find. She had such strong hopes of finding what she wanted in San Francisco even if she did not know exactly what she was seeking. Yet why should she go there when she had just met the perfect man here? Was not the east coast superior to the west? Was not Yale superior in prestige to any school the west could boast? Was not New Haven a thousand miles closer to the family farm in Maumee than was San Francisco? Linc claimed he wanted to help her reach San Francisco. Was it a noble gesture, or was he selfishly seeking to get her away from the presence of a man he did not like? She had trouble discerning Linc's true motives, his real goals.

Goals. John pursued a splendid goal, a prestigious position at Yale. Linc pursued none, save the nebulous wish perhaps someday to emigrate to a foreign country. John was a man of purpose and breeding. Linc was a wanderer and half-breed, his future as blemished as his past by his mixed heritage. John was unflappably suave and sophisticated; Linc could be the crudest person north of the equator, Felicidad's opinion of him notwithstanding.

She pictured life with John—elegant clothes, stylish parties, conversation with the very best minds in the country (nay, in the world!), prestige and, frankly, no small splash of glamour. John seemed reluctant to commit himself fully to God, or to give full credit to God, but he certainly knew all about the faith even if he was critical of its precepts. He would come around, given time and Naomi's good example.

What would life with Linc be? No ease—hardship was pretty well guaranteed. No silks and satins—that, too, was guaranteed. No . . . but wait! Linc spoke of sending her to San Francisco. He compared her lot with that of a Navajo squaw. He championed her right to choose her own destiny, though she was strong-willed enough to need no champion. But never had he mentioned anything at all about marriage.

What was his interest in her? Apparently, nothing strong

131

enough to encourage a marriage proposal motivated him. Most important, he was a heathen, an infidel, an unbeliever. Paul in his second letter to the Corinthians sternly warned against being unequally yoked with an unbeliever. John at least confessed the faith. How closely he followed it was his own affair; he was a responsible adult.

The choice this morning seemed so abundantly clear. Naomi could no longer understand why there had ever been any question. She would go down to the latrine—nature was calling urgently now. When she returned to breakfast, John would be properly apologetic about disturbing her last night. If he did not discuss the matter further this morning, he would surely do so at some other time.

And what if he was uncertain about courting her? His friction with Linc served Naomi's purposes well. As Linc obstinately opposed John's right to demand her hand, John would all the more insist upon it. Neither of them need know she was making her choice now, this morning. And when John made a formal and proper proposal (he of all people knew what was formal and proper!), she would accept it formally and properly.

She stood up and started down the hill, down the loose and gravelly ridge. The day was clearing, the mists disappearing. Her mind had cleared also, and felt as cheerfully sunny as the morning. She had cleared up any confusion. She made her choice.

She chose John.

When John first set up this camp, he selected the location of the latrine well. In a small gully well away from camp, it was enclosed by rocks and thickets on all sides. It helps to have a pleasant and private nook for answering personal needs.

She completed the needs of the moment. Then, in full sun, she took her time wending her way back up the steep hill. Customarily she devoted her first walk of the morning to prayer. She had been negligent in prayer of late, pressed by all the strange events of this unimaginable journey. She had much for which to give thanks, from safety to weather. She strolled, in no hurry. The morning itself felt too good to rush through, as did prayer time.

One second she was enjoying the crisp air and soothing sun. The next, her mouth and nose were clamped shut by what felt like a massive bear paw, and she was being dragged backwards. She struggled automatically, but it did no good. She tried to pry the fingers loose; she couldn't breathe. She estimated approximately where her attacker's eyes ought to be and tried to reach back far enough to gouge them, but his iron arm clamped around hers and held them down. Perhaps she could kick a sensitive spot, uncouth as the idea might be. But her legs were no longer strong enough.

The struggling abated against her will. Terrified, she watched the beige rocks and blue sky fade casually to darkness. Then the terror faded away as well.

CHAPTER 15

HER MOUTH SEEMED full of cotton, but at least she could breathe again. She felt all disoriented and upside down. No wonder. As her wits came wandering home bit by bit, she eventually determined she was, in fact, upside down. Her abductors had draped her over the saddle of a moving horse. Her legs dangled down the right side, her arms dangled down the left, and her cheek splacked against a stirrup leather. She raised her head enough to keep her cheek from thumping. They had bound her wrists together with a pigging string, a rawhide thong cowboys and herders carry for arcane purposes. Her hands were swelling and turning purple. The rag they had placed in her mouth tasted cotton. She loathed to think how filthy her gag might be. However horrible, it was there to stay. They had anchored it firmly with a kerchief tied about her head and mouth. She tried to manipulate it with her tongue and nearly gagged.

She must be on Neeskah's horse. Roan hide flexed beyond her right arm. And she discerned Nizhoni's charcoal gray shoulder beyond her.

She might break her neck in the next few moments, but the chance was worth taking. Almost anything would be better than this drastic discomfort. She arched her back quickly and got her elbows under her. Pushing and wiggling, she slid legs-first off the saddle. She plopped into the hard dirt and sat quietly a moment until some of that extra blood left her head.

Neeskah had been riding up behind his saddle. She did not understand his barrage of Navajo except to discern that it was not complimentary. The only word she recognized was *belagana*, the somewhat derogatory Navajo term for an Anglo. He slid off and stomped over to her. Joe Dasanie rode in beside her on Nizhoni, smirking. Was he sniggering at her or at his perturbed partner? The sling which had been cradling his arm was filthy.

She grunted as clearly as possible (not clearly at all) and pointed to her mouth.

Dasanie said something terse and Neeskah whined. Neeskah gripped her arm to pull her to her feet. She looped her bound arms over her knees and tucked her head into a tight, stubborn little ball. There was more Navajo grumbling. Neeskah loosened the kerchief, and Naomi lost no time spitting out the wad of cotton fabric which proved to be another handkerchief. She dared not ponder its history.

She bolted to her feet. She really ought to be terribly afraid, and in a way she was, but anger crowded the fear aside. "I will thank you two persons—for gentlemen you are not—to unbind my hands as well, before they turn black and drop off."

Neeskah grabbed her arm and gave her a yank toward his horse. "Up!"

She jerked away from him. "I am not a sack of flour to be pushed and shoved and slung about."

Dasanie said something which caused derisive amusement. Naomi might not be a sack of flour, but Neeskah pushed and shoved anyway. He didn't bother to let her mount as properly and gracefully as possible. He hoisted her roughly in an upward direction and let her scramble into the saddle as best she could, using only purple stumps for hands. He swung up behind her. At least now she was riding upright and could breathe through her mouth. She had best not say too much more, lest they stuff that rag back in.

She fumed. She feared. She worried. Surely John and Linc would both come charging to her aid; ideally they would join forces in a well-orchestrated and successful rescue attempt. But they had practically scratched each other's eyes out last night. More realistically, therefore, she could expect them to squabble about the best course of action (and that without her mitigating influence), shout each other down, perhaps even come to blows. Certainly neither would cheerfully cooperate, let alone obey the other. Men! They could well get hurt simply through their lack of cooperation. These two Indians were not fools. She was at once afraid John and Linc would come for her and also afraid they would not.

As her anger subsided, cold fear burgeoned. In that first encounter, Dasanie had expressed a general bitterness and avowed to hurt John by hurting her. Linc seemed to find the bitterness easy to understand; so it must be real. Dasanie's evil purposes were now multiplied, for he had a score to settle with Linc as well. Indeed, his arm seemed to be very painful even yet; he would let Nizhoni's reins drape loose on the horse's neck in order to support his arm with his free hand. All in all, the chances of maintaining her personal moral integrity looked pitifully slim.

She was bait, of course, the lure to draw John and Linc into ambush. Surely both of them were too smart to walk into a trap. But there was also the matter of Nizhoni. Naomi notwithstanding, Linc would certainly tackle these two just to get his horse back.

If ever there were a time for prayer, this was it. Yet, now when she needed communion with God most, she could not marshal prayer. She could not envision how God could possibly intercede effectively, even if in theory nothing was impossible for Him. He could not even strike these two miscreants with lightning, since she could find no clouds in the azure sky. The dearth of prayer frustrated her, and the frustration magnified her fear.

They rode without rest all morning. When Neeskah's horse flagged, Naomi was switched to Nizhoni's back awhile. They stopped somewhere around noon (the sun was at its highest), mostly for the horses' sake. Apparently there was no food. Naomi was hungry, having missed breakfast, and outrageously thirsty. The one blessing of this respite was that they untied her wrists. At last she could hang on when the riding got rough.

By midafternoon they had wound through a tangle of confusing low hills and crossed a low, flat valley. Directly ahead loomed another of those ubiquitous mesas which separated this country into two discreet worlds—UpThere and DownHere. Both worlds seemed fairly similar—flat or gently rolling desert—but for one major difference. Virtually inaccessible, UpThere perched on pedestals of sheer vertical rock often hundreds of feet high.

The horses' feet gritched in loose gravel as they wound along the base of this mesa's pedestal. Naomi twisted in her seat behind Joe Dasanie and craned her neck, but she could not see the top of the cliff. Were they going to negotiate some mysterious passageway leading upward, perhaps from there to pour boiling oil on their enemies? They turned aside suddenly into a narrow split in the cliff face, an exceedingly strait defile. From a quarter mile away, Naomi would never have suspected it was there.

Its floor was sandy wash, its walls nearly vertical. They closed in on her. Impulsively she stretched out both arms. Her fingertips came within a yard of touching the rock wall on either side. She could just imagine being caught in a flash flood here. And flash floods did happen; proof was in the dried grass tufts and other debris that hung here and there, snagged twenty feet up the canyon wall.

The dry stream bed at their feet twisted this way and that. The floor of the canyon was by turns rocky and precipitous or smooth and sandy. The horses seemed to stumble as much in the sand as in the rocks. They must be very weary. She was forced to cling for dear life to the despicable Joe Dasanie as the horses clambered up a waterless waterfall.

The gorge widened slightly to perhaps twenty feet across. Just ahead a boulder pile nearly blocked it. Dasanie stopped at the base of the rocks and shouted a greeting upward. The boulders responded in Navajo. An iron-hard face popped out; a Navajo stood on top of the rocks, a man even more dangerous-looking than Dasanie. These two were not alone! And Linc and John assumed they were!

The chasm widened further into a proper canyon; the walls were as steep yet, but not so high. They must have climbed quickly.

The gloom of the narrow defile brightened instantly. The horses stopped. Naomi peered over Dasanie's shoulder. They had ridden out into a grassy meadow a quarter mile long and perhaps two-thirds wide. Sheer cliffs ten to thirty feet high surrounded the meadow, boxed it in, cut it off. The meadow was neither UpThere nor DownHere. It hung suspended in solid rock, protected and isolated. Naomi had heard of box canyons before, but she never dreamed they could be this dramatic.

138

Here at the lower end, the walls were highest. The stream bed tumbled, dry, into the narrow canyon. Three hundred feet upstream a little clump of reeds promised surface water. The flat floor was carpeted in grass a foot high. The wind rippled it with wavy undulations. Clumps of mesquite trees huddled along one wall from this end to the far end. The walls at the far end were lowest—perhaps twice a man's height—and another crack in the rocks snaked straight up through the wall at the far end. It did not seem to be a way out; they had just entered by the only door.

The canyon might be isolated, but it was not uninhabited. She saw no sturdy wooden winter hogans, but she counted two summer style stick-and-brush hogans—no, three. A horizontal pall of smoke hung above their heads, so someone lived in at least some of these shelters. A half-dozen horses stood about or nibbled at the grass on the far side of the wash.

An Indian stepped out of the mesquite a hundred yards away and cradled his rifle on his arm. Here came another. Within moments four rough-and-tough-looking men stood around her horse. Dasanie threw his leg over the saddle horn and slid to the ground.

The men seemed primarily interested in Nizhoni. They nodded and grunted as they studied him, apparently discussing his better points. One man ran a hand across his rump and pulled the tail aside for a posterior inspection.

One fellow nearly six feet tall (but not nearly so slim as Linc) looked Naomi over in the same way he had eyed the horse. He evaluated her bust, her waist, her hips. He looked at her exposed ankle. He picked up her hem for a better look at her calf. Without thinking, she swatted him with the hard romal.

A tiny shiver of panic ran down her back. She should not have done that, at least not so hard. The man's face tightened in surprise and instant anger. Dasanie spoke and everyone laughed. They were laughing at her imprudence, she could tell. No matter—better they laugh at her than become angry with her. The men babbled together several minutes. Were they talking about her? About John? She couldn't tell.

Dasanie yanked the reins out of her hands and flipped the loop forward over Nizhoni's ears. He led the gray horse the length of the meadow, with Naomi displayed in the saddle like some sort of war prize. Is that what she was?

They stopped near mesquites at the head of the valley. Neeskah was already there beside an unkempt summer hogan. He climbed stiffly, wearily off his horse. Naomi realized the man was probably much older than she would have first guessed. He stared a moment at the blackened fire ring in front of the hogan and wandered off, gathering sticks, leaves and branches for a fire.

Dasanie ambled over to the fire ring and stretched out beside it in the grass. He drew a deep breath and cradled his head with his good hand. "Unsaddle and bring our gear over here to the fire," he ordered Naomi. "Don' bother tie the horses. Turn 'em loose. Ain' going nowhere."

"I am not your slave."

"That's what you think. You my woman now." He smirked, a maddening curl in his lip. "You get use to it. Pretty soon you like it, won' want nobody else. Jus' wait 'n see. Now get busy."

So she was a trophy, stripped from an Anglo's hands, stolen from a breed who had cast his lot with his white side. She started to fumble for a stirrup, stopped and perched back securely in her seat.

"You've never been to Bosque Redondo, have you?" she asked.

He raised his head to stare at her. "So what?"

140

"Mr. Rawlin's mother was there until she married. No, I guess she married before she got there, but she walked most of the trail. Not all the Dineh were rounded up and interned. Some were left behind. Like you."

"You talking about that breed, eh?"

"No, about you. He claimed a few Dineh held out like the Apaches have been holding out. Still rebelling, still fighting the Anglos. He says there aren't many left and they don't dare tackle the Anglos much any more. But they're outlaws all the same. Outlaws toward the Anglos and outlaws toward the Dineh too."

"Some Dineh still got pride."

"Why should you be proud about killing your own blood? I know a woman named Doli, a very lonely woman with a little boy. Her husband died by your hand, or the hand of one of your chums here. I'm sure she's not the only one who's suffering years of loneliness and grief because of you."

"I din' tell you talk. I said tend the horses."

"Linc says there aren't many of you left—many of the old outlaws—but I'd have guessed there were more of you than these pitiful few. How many did I count, four plus you two? Where did they go off to; have they joined the Apaches?"

"'Paches, Utes, Yaquis. Mostly down to Mexico. Gone. Not home. This is home here. The Dineh living and the Dineh dead, they all here. Not some'eres else. We aren' the only ones. There's others other places. We ain' all."

She twisted on her perch to look down the boxed-in valley. She listened. A desert sparrow, a little black-throated songster, chirped from some low, woody bushes near the wash. In the distance a horse sneezed. That was all. She turned back to Dasanie. "No children. No women."

"Not no more. Maybe I share you 'round a little."

141

The horses both dropped their heads to rip and bite at the tough grass. Naomi could steal Nizhoni here and ride right out of this valley, but that watchman on the boulders would stop her. Even if she slipped past him, perhaps catching him by surprise, Nizhoni was too tired to go far or fast. They would recapture her at their leisure and Nizhoni might even drop over in the attempt. Besides, where could she run? She had no idea within thirty miles where she was exactly. These men were intimately familiar with the country, stone by stone. She would have to make the best of things and wait. Perhaps escape might be practical later.

Where were Linc and John? Naomi hoped they were calmly and quickly gathering help from sources of some sort. Linc mentioned settlers near Moenkopi; might they go there for help? But that was likely only wishful thinking. She was a more practical person than to dream such things. In reality, she knew they would be on their way here. They would ride up that canyon, not suspecting this nest of hardened raiders. Like sheep to the slaughter, they were hastening to their deaths.

CHAPTER 16

You can watch a million cows being milked. But until you have taken the udder in your own hands and received some instruction, you will never properly milk a cow. You can watch a million faithful souls at prayer, but that will not help you pray. It was strange, Naomi thought, how her mind was still capable of logical deduction, even under these mean circumstances.

She had seen horses saddled and unsaddled by the score. From the shelter of that overhang she had watched Linc Rawlins saddle this very horse before her. But that didn't make the job a bit easier. The cinch was secured by a strange double half-hitch sort of knot. Even after she figured it out, her fingers were almost too weak to loosen it.

She would serve faithfully and tend these horses only because she was compelled by Scripture. She was to perform every service as if it were for Jesus—and in a sense it was—but her carnal self rebelled at the notion. Serve these brigands? She would rather serve Nizhoni. In a sense she was doing that too. She scratched him under his jaw, the place he couldn't scratch on his own.

Finally she pulled Nizhoni's bridle up over his ears. He spit out the bit, pivoted away from her, and trotted off. She left the saddles in an untidy pile to watch the horses.

Nizhoni stopped at the sandy wash. He ambled down to the reed thicket. Apparently he found open water and drank deeply; his head was low for several minutes. He walked upstream a few feet. Suddenly his knees buckled. Naomi gasped; he had drunk too much cold water and now was cramping! But no—no, he wanted only to roll in the warm loose sand. He flung himself onto his back. He squirmed. He twisted his head around to rub his graceful neck in the dirt. He kicked to midway, flailing his stockinged legs straight up, then flopped over to repeat the whole joyous adventure. He was reveling in comfort and freedom. Did he miss Linc? Did he dream even remotely that his true master was approaching mortal danger right now? Did he appreciate the quiet beauty of this secluded spot? Like all horses, Nizhoni did not seem to discern whether his riders be good or evil. Too many men were similarly unconcerned about ethics, Naomi mused.

Neeskah's ragged roan watched the performance a moment, then wandered out into the wash to find his own sandy spot. Compared with the sleek and clever Nizhoni, the other pony seemed a dull imitation of a horse.

Enough of this idle wool-gathering! Naomi snapped her attentions back to Dasanie. "I assume a meal of some sort is forthcoming. I'm dreadfully hungry. I've not eaten all day."

"You get use to that too. Cooking's squaw work. We jus' waiting for you finish there."

"Ah yes. Division of labor." She plopped down across the fire ring from Dasanie and folded her hands in her lap.

She basked in the sheer pleasure of sitting upon solid, unmoving ground. "I understand in the Navajo culture that possessions are owned individually. For example, I understand that if a horse belongs to a man's wife, it's hers and she rides it. He walks. If it belongs to him, he rides and she walks. Is that correct?"

Neeskah was back, his arms full of firewood of all sizes. He dropped the scraggly bundle and wandered off to the hogan.

She looked Dasanie in the eye. "Very well. I wish to thank you both for the gift of your horses. Since I have ridden both, and now am caring for both of them, the implication is obvious. They're mine. A generous gesture. I'll try not to let the fact that at least one is stolen bother me."

Neeskah turned to stare; he'd bought it.

Dasanie laughed. "You stole mine."

"Hardly. You could have had it back for the asking. John was all ready to trade your horse for Linc's, but I'm sure you're too smart for that. You made much the better deal; Nizhoni's twice the horse your bay nag is."

"Nizhoni, eh? You such good friends with that breed you know his horse by name." Dasanie wiggled a finger. "Come 'ere."

A calm mien now would serve well. "Are you familiar with the concept of guardian angels?"

"Angels. Spirits?"

"Of a sort. Non-corporeal; by that I mean no fleshly bodies. But they're real, all the same. The Bible promises that angels have charge over us to protect us. I trust that promise, Joe Dasanie. You can't touch me unless God lets you. I've put my trust in Him through Jesus and He takes care of me."

Dasanie frowned. "Now tha's new." He snorted. "I touch you anytime I please."

She shrugged. "I'll not argue. I've said what I said. However, you're too smart to spoil me. You want me as a hostage—a bargaining tool—and I'm worth much more in, ah, an unbesmirched condition. Untouched. That's the word. You've gone to considerable trouble to bring me here. You want a maximum return on your investment of time and effort. Therefore, I assume it is both God's will and yours that I remain undefiled." She was amazed by her own boldness. She hoped the exterior presented the desired appearance of unruffled calm. The interior was an apsen leaf in a high wind.

She had best back up her bravado with concentrated prayer. She was putting her Lord on the line and she hated to. What if . . . ? Dasanie stared at her. He stared and stared.

She could not sit still. She stood up casually, deliberately, and stretched her back. To rid herself of some of this tension, she scanned the canyon walls by eye, picturing possible routes up the sheer faces—if she were a goat, that is. The cliffs looked exactly like the cliffs everywhere else, and nowhere did she see any climbable routes up.

John's lectures had made some effect; she recognized sedimentary rock now. Weathering revealed at least two distinct layers just in the cliffs at the end of the valley. She walked twenty feet out from the trees to look more closely. She found a break in the mesquite thickets and moved in closer, reviewing mentally what John had said.

The nearer she came and the closer she looked, the better it appeared. She walked quickly back to Joe Dasanie. "John told you what to look for when seeking fossil strata. Isn't that the very thing he was talking about, up there? Come look. Please." She hurried back down to her vantage point from which to examine the innocuous strip of dirty rock.

Curiosity won. Dasanie lurched to his feet and came shuffling over.

146

She pointed. "See? Look past that grayish stone up there. And the off-colored lumps and nodules. And that sort of line right there. Exactly what John was talking about, don't you agree? You have a real find here! John will be so pleased."

Dasanie sniggered. "He don' be much pleased when he get here. 'Sides, he's looking for gold, not bones."

She turned to him. "I don't know where you get that notion. Stop and think. If he were seeking gold, he'd have explained to you and Neeskah how to recognize gold-bearing rock. And I'm sure you must know that gold is found in igneous deposits such as those occurring west and south of here. Or at least in quartz intrusions and there's none of that sort of thing around this area." She would not have thought she could remember Linc's casual geology lesson. Or perhaps she didn't remember it and had gotten it all wrong. The blank look on Dasanie's face told her it didn't matter.

"You as bad as he is."

"It's all so very simple. John is here looking for layered formations like these. He works for a professor back east who's simply daft over dinosaur fossils. You see, John wants to be a professor also, and he's literally buying his way into favor with old bones. Do you realize how much John's employer will pay for a find like this? And Yale has enough money to support a whole museum full of such bones. You've heard John mention Peabody Museum. There's your gold, Dasanie, right up there."

The Indian studied her and she tried to meet his eye calmly. He shook his head. "Huh-uh. Maybe you believe him, but not me. It's not bones he wants—it's gold."

She wagged her head. "Back in Toledo some of the bigger boys would make sport of the little ones—especially the poor children. They would throw a shiny penny down on the ground beside a dull old nickel. Then they'd laugh as the

147

children scrambled for the penny and ignored the nickel, just because the penny was prettier. It looked more valuable. You're doing exactly the same thing. You're ignoring that dull old nickel up there in your search for a shiny penny.''

Dasanie was standing right at her elbow, pressing close. "How long he say them bones been there?''

"Millions of years, at least. So he claims.''

"Then they pretty well stuck there. Won't go nowhere. Got plenty time. I got other things I wanna do now.'' He reached out with his good arm and brushed his folded finger down her cheek. "Come 'ere.''

What she had dreaded was about to happen. She took a step backward involuntarily and mentally redoubled her prayers for angelic protection. Her breath faltered.

From the far distance down in the canyon a poor-will whistled faintly.

Dasanie glanced off in that direction and smiled. "Tha's the lookout. He sees your lovers. They in the canyon.''

"How does he know who they are?''

"Only strangers would come here, them two. The others, they take care of 'em. I told you do something. Do it.''

Her heart thumped. Surely Linc and John recognized the danger of entering that narrow canyon, of approaching a fastness of this sort. She was impressed with their resolve to rescue her, but this was foolish. She could cry out and warn them, but that would only make things worse. They would hear her and hasten faster to fall victim. She clamped her lips tight. Never had she felt so helpless.

Dasanie took a step still closer and she took two quick steps back. That instant, before she could begin to collect her thoughts, Dasanie crashed flat to the ground beneath a huge, sheepskin-covered pile. From nowhere—from above—from heaven—Linc Rawlins had dropped in.

She gasped, thunderstruck. "How did . . . where did . . . ?"

Pigging strings must be basic equipment in this country; Linc had one too. He whipped it out of his back pocket and wrenched Dasanie's bad arm behind his back. Naomi winced. Linc twisted the good wrist back and bound them together.

He stood up straight and arched his back. "Getting too old for this kinda stuff." He pointed upstream. "Beyond that dry waterfall there's enough breaks in the cliff that we can climb up and out. Let's go." He grabbed her wrist and started off.

"But what about Nizhoni?"

"I'll get him later."

She dug her heels in and dragged him to a stop. "No! The lookout downcanyon whistled that someone was coming. John is coming and he's in grave danger. We must warn him; save him!"

He yanked her into motion again. "We're not abandoning your bone-digger. He'll come just far enough to draw their attention. Give me time to get you out. Will you hurry?"

"But John is . . ."

"John's gonna meet us at Winwaddie Rock. He knows where it is." Linc was at a full run now, hunched over to slip under the mesquite limbs. Naomi had to duck too; she wanted to slow down and Linc wouldn't let her.

They darted to the creek and clambered up a ledge. He planted his palms firmly on her backside. With both hands he boosted her up onto a high ledge. Then he came popping up behind her.

"Don't stop; keep going!"

She should climb and not talk. Still, "How did you find me so quickly? This canyon is so well hidden. And all these Indians . . ."

149

"John woke me up soon as he realized you were gone. Southern Pacific Railroad doesn't lay tracks any easier'n yours to follow. They wanted us to track you here. Up! Hustle!"

"It's a trap, of course." She squirmed on her belly to climb higher.

"We know it. That's why John . . ."

A gunshot loud enough to rouse the dead echoed up and down the rock walls and jangled their ears. Naomi gasped and Linc wheeled. Behind them, far away and far down at the base of that dry rockfall, Neeskah pointed John's gun toward heaven.

Neeskah waved the gun barrel. "Back down. It's over."

Naomi reflected, abstractly, how high they had climbed. She looked behind them, up the rocky little crack in the world, at how far short they were of safety.

She sighed heavily. "At least, if John comes no closer, he probably is safe. No gunshots in the lower canyon."

Neeskah was laughing. "We got your bone-digger, little lady, and we got your lover, and we got you. How good you stay, that's how safe your lovers stay. Got me?"

She understood all right. She glanced up at Linc. The happy tilt of his eyes was spoiled by anger, perhaps even hatred. Naomi thought of Jesus' story about the man who was rid of one demon only to play host to seven.

She knew how he felt.

CHAPTER 17

"EYES ARE THE WINDOWS of the soul," Naomi's mother always said. Perhaps so, but they were no clear window on a person's thoughts. Naomi watched Linc's eyes for some hint, any hint at all, of what he might be thinking. He had turned as hard and stony as the rock walls around them. Was he considering running? Apparently. Was he enraged? Definitely. She could read that much.

He gripped her hand to help her thread her way downstream. His massive strength poured through his hand into hers. But coming down the steep and ragged incline was, if anything, harder than climbing up. She hopped and jumped and managed to reach the bottom without breaking any bones. Linc negotiated the whole drop, not once taking his eyes off Neeskah.

Naomi stood up beside Neeskah, brushed off her skirt. Someday she'd burn these dirty clothes. "You said you had John. Where is he?"

Neeskah was watching Linc's final descent. "Try to jump

me, you don' reach ground alive. Go 'head. Try. Give me a excuse, big man.''

"I said, 'Where's John'?''

"Down the canyon taking a little nap. Go see." Neeskah seemed pleased as punch.

She cast one last long look at Linc, turned and ran downstream, down the length of the meadow. They were watching her. They were all watching her, she knew. She ran out of breath before she reached the canyon and slowed to a walk. Long prickly grass awns stuck in her skirt and stockings. She knew also that Linc's lot would not be comfortable. Someone was releasing Joe Dasanie by now. He would not treat Linc gently and thoughtfully. She regretted very much that Linc had become entangled so disastrously in her life. And yet she was so happy and relieved that he was here, that she was no longer alone.

She walked from sunshine into gloom and started down the narrow canyon. There was that boulder pile up ahead (or rather, down ahead), and there stood the lookout atop it, watching her. And here was John, sprawled on his back on this side of the boulders. He lay in the sand, white and still. He had come much further up the canyon than she would have expected were he following the plan Linc described.

She didn't know what to do. She sat down close beside him. She remembered the sense of doom—of fear and dread—that slammed her when she saw Dasanie ride away on Nizhoni. She remembered her consternation when Linc was hurt. Why did she not feel just as badly now—for John? She saw no blood anywhere and had heard no shots. Therefore, to employ the vernacular, the lookout must have coldcocked him in passing. Head injuries are serious, very serious. And the head of a college professor with John's gifts was especially precious. She took the limp hand in hers and held it for lack of any more productive thing to do. She wished she could develop more emotional travail over his sorry state. Think of the grief and pain she could have saved everybody had she only been content to remain in Santa Fe, at least until the end of the school term. She could have saved even more grief by never having left Ohio at all. But exotic Santa Fe had seemed so alluring, and now here she was. No doubt much of that allure came from the fact that her three best friends in normal school had planned to travel to New Mexico; it seemed natural, then, for her to come along. Ah, how sorry for herself she felt!

She felt sorrier for John than for herself. All he wanted was to complete his survey and hie himself back east where he belonged. And yet he did fit comfortably out here. He rose above his circumstances here; no doubt he did so wherever he found himself. What a magnificent man! Why did she not fear for his health and comfort more? That bothered her. He was beginning to stir. He'd wake up soon.

She felt sorriest of all for Linc. In his own unpolished way, he was a gentleman of sorts. He might not treat her like a lady, but he treated her tenderly and well. And look at the harvest he had reaped for his attempt to help her!

She found herself near tears again. Well, she should be more diligent in her praying. She closed her burning eyes to address the Father. It seemed so far that the more she prayed, the worse the troubles got. Still, that was no reason to stop . . .

Her eyes popped open. What was she thinking?! Not one of her prayers had gone unanswered. It was simply that the answers were not exactly what she expected. She almost smiled as she thought of Linc dropping out of nowhere just as Dasanie's lust surfaced. Her God was a God of "Nicks of Time," but He certainly was not ignoring her petitions.

She saw now new avenues of prayer, and she had best

explore them properly—and swiftly. She laid John's pale and flaccid hand across his breast and twisted around to a position of prayer on her knees. John might well awaken and see her and ridicule. So be it. To this point she had been praying moment-to-moment, as if she knew what was best and need only make a list for God to follow. That was all backwards. God knew best, and she must follow His direction. She must follow and stop trying to lead.

She thanked God profusely for their deliverance thus far. She asked for Linc's conversion and John's enlightenment. And now she asked that she be used in whatever way God thought best. Live or die, she would reflect His Son. She would . . .

A stone rattled upstream. Neeskah and Linc came around the bend into full view. Linc stopped cold to stare at her. Was prayer so terribly unusual? To a pagan it probably was, but he seemed somehow astounded. She broke off prayer until later when she could again concentrate. She stood up.

Linc glared at his prostrated partner in rescue, looked off toward the boulders. "He was supposed to come a couple hundred yards, make some noise, and skin back out."

"Perhaps he simply misjudged the distance."

"He couldn't stand taking orders from a breed with a third-grade education."

"I don't want to hear the pot calling the kettle black. You would have just as much trouble following a plan of his devising. Maybe more. City slickers can't know anything practical."

He looked at her and his eyes regained some of their tilt. His face softened; in fact he almost smiled. Then Neeskah jabbed him into action. Linc scooped John up onto his shoulder and had nearly carried him to the hidden valley before John regained his wits enough to walk on his own. Naomi followed with her feet, but her fancies flew

154

elsewhere. As they walked back up the meadow past those pairs of eyes, she considered her new approach to prayer. And she looked again at the bedding layer. It extended the length of the valley.

Linc cooked that night and seemed happy for something to keep him busy. John made critical remarks about men's work and women's, but Naomi was glad Linc took the job. She had no idea what to do with the wormy cornmeal Neeskah borrowed from friends, and Linc made it into very tasty flatcakes.

Naomi had hoped nightfall in this secluded little canyon would somehow differ from nightfall out in the vastness of the open desert. It did not. The same closed-in feeling came upon her, despite that they were already closed in by uncompromising rock walls. And for all its greater size, Neeskah and Dasanie's campfire did not make a circle of light much larger than did John's little coal oil lamp.

John tried valiantly to remain alert. He squirmed and shifted. But the trying day and the lump on the back of his head took their toll. His eyelids drooped to half-mast and before long he had dozed off, his chin on his chest.

Naomi stood up and stretched. The night was turning colder. She laid a couple more dry mesquite limbs on the fire and sat down cross-legged before it. It occurred to her she should have deliberately seated herself beside John, since he was her choice. Instead she found herself sitting nearer Linc than John. She poked the fire a little just to watch the sparks dance. Her thoughts were becoming confused again, a churning melange of ideas intruding upon one another. She looked at Linc. He wasn't dozing. He studied the fire with eyes snapping as bright as the flames. Now and then his lips tightened.

He broke the silence so unexpectedly she jumped, startled, though his voice was little more than a mumble. "You were praying there, in the canyon. You don't need a church for that kind of stuff?''

"One sits at a dining table to eat, but one may eat without sitting at the table.''

"You make church and religion sound like two different things.''

"In a way they are. A lot of people go to church simply because it seems to be the thing to do, and not because they truly want to worship God. Church is an important part of the faith—corporate worship—but it's only part, not parcel.''

He slipped back within himself again, thinking.

John stirred, watched the fire a few minutes and drifted off again. Even folded in that cramped position asleep, he was massively handsome. The slithering fire made him glow, golden.

She was getting cold despite the fire. She rearranged her cape and tried to snuggle deeper into it. Without so much as looking at her, Linc extended his arm and pulled her in against his side. He rubbed her shoulder a moment, preoccupied, then retracted his arm. She might not feel much warmer for his gesture, but she felt much better. The crowding darkness did not press so ominously. Despite all the unpleasantness in this situation, a delightful romantic feeling washed over her. Absurd, to think of romance now, with John asleep and Linc ignoring her.

She tried to sort her muddled thoughts, but they were hopelessly tangled. Of all the random things popping in and out her mind, one question stood out prominently and only Linc could answer it.

"Linc? Understand it's none of my business. But I must know anyway. About you and Doli. Are you two, . . . I mean . . . do you two ever . . . uh . . . you know.''

"You're right—it's none of your business.'' He glanced at her briefly. "Yeah. We—know each other.''

156

"I guess you were getting to know each other even better the day I was there."

He smiled. "Kinda thought you might be peeking." The smile faded. "No. Not that day. I had it in mind, and so did she. So we took a little walk out to the hay shed to check on her hay supply. But all I could think about was how you behaved yourself. How you didn't even want to look like you were thinking about sinning, and it wasn't just for appearances either. As it ended up, all we did was check her hay supply and came in. Didn't get around to anything serious."

"I didn't think it was that cardinal a sin in the Navajo culture; I mean, not with a widow."

"You forget Lincoln was a man of God. Pa brought me up knowing right from wrong. Maybe it wasn't all that wrong for Doli, but it was for me. I guess you'd call it an attack of conscience. You reminded me too much of my father's high principles."

"Is that bad?"

"I consider you a good influence. That should please you."

"I didn't know you considered me at all."

"Ever since I first scooped you off that hill, I haven't done anything else but. Scares me; woman never got under my skin like this before."

"I rather thought you'd marry Doli, settle down. It's logical, when you think about it."

"Logical maybe, but I was never in love with her. Not like Pa loved Ma—ready to give up everything for her if he had to."

Naomi bit her lip. Linc was giving up everything for her—his horse, perhaps even his life. And he was not her choice. So far she had not returned so much as the most basic amenity. "I never did thank you properly for all your

157

efforts on my behalf. You're most generous and noble about this whole business.''

He studied her so intently she cringed. "And what exactly is a proper thank you?''

"Why, to say thank you. I deeply appreciate your sacrifices and . . . including Nizhoni . . . and . . . the words, I suppose. Thank you.''

"Actions speak louder than words.''

"That's true. Saint James in his epistle says 'faith without works is dead.' That's why I try so hard to . . .'' She stopped.

His gaze was not a leer, nor was it remotely derogatory. His eyes had regained that old twinkle, and the mischievous tilt had returned. He was scheming; his mind could skate circles around hers when he chose.

She sat up straight. "Just what do you intend . . .''

The long arm swung out unannounced and enveloped her. His mouth was on hers. Suddenly she was encased, firmly and deliciously. Like a fool she fought him, but only for a moment until she realized what she was doing. She was warm again, or perhaps she no longer noticed the cold. His ardor melted her into him as candle wax melts into fabric—totally, irrevocably. The urgency of his kiss pressed her cheek and chin into that soft, bulky sheepskin collar.

What if John awoke? And surely Dasanie was watching; the lecher missed nothing. And what if . . . but who cared? She matched his kiss, lips for lips, breath for breath, and the rest of the world slunk away. She felt disappointed and vaguely cheated when he eventually released her.

He unwrapped and parked his elbows on his knees. "You're welcome.''

He seemed not the least affected, but it rendered her speechless. Very rarely did anything at all ever do that. Her thoughts jumbled into a worse tangle than ever. She would wait for some other time—some propitious moment in the future perhaps a long time hence—to explain to Linc why she had chosen John.

CHAPTER 18

DAWN COULD NOT COME too soon. The captives had to sleep sitting by the fire as Neeskah and Dasanie took turns enjoying peaceful slumber in warm bedrolls within the brush hogan. Naomi woke at first light and spent a good hour pacing back and forth beside the fire, trying to bring life to her toes and fingers.

John awoke quite cross and huddled, scowling at the embers. Linc, ever practical, swiped some dry branches from the wall of the hogan. He fanned the modest pile of coals into a welcome blaze and hunkered down beside it.

Linc glanced at Naomi. "Been wondering something."

"What?"

"School year runs from, say, September through spring."

"Usually."

"You're a schoolteacher, you said. But you left to go traveling in the middle of a school year. Why?"

"Very perceptive. Now how do I phrase this politely? A highly paid executive in the school system became exces-

160

sively enamored of me. He promised numerous blessings for my favors and various hardships if they were withheld. When he pressed his suit too strongly, San Francisco beckoned."

"His wife is a shrew who can't stand him."

"His wife is a very nice lady. He's just that sort of person, unfortunately. I wasn't the first."

"Did ya like teaching there?"

"Oh, my, yes. The children were a joy."

"And you left it all just to protect your honor."

"'Just'? Hardly. You see, God sacrificed much for me. The very least I can do is forego something as temporal as a teaching position."

His dark eyes tried to see into her mind. "I guess that's putting your theology on the line."

"Some theology, I suppose. Book learning. But it's more practical than that. I don't want to displease God. Also, whatever I do and say in public reflects on Him, since I claim to be His. What would you think of Jesus if I became adulterously involved with the likes of that person? You see? It's a responsibility which I accepted when I accepted His grace."

"So when you left New Mexico, God's honor was at stake as much as yours."

She cocked her head. "Essentially."

John straightened a little. "What became of your class? Surely you didn't just walk out on it."

"Yes, I did. The aforementioned executive is paid a handsome sum to handle that sort of thing. I saw no disgrace in leaving him with a problem of his own making."

"I'm disappointed in you, Naomi. I should think you'd have a much better sense of responsibility." John was frowning—sulking.

Why should that irritate her? John was right in a way.

161

"My first responsibility is always to God. It seemed appropriate action at the time, and I'd do it again."

"That hardly absolves your responsi—"

"Get off her!" Linc snapped it so viciously that John stopped, mostly in surprise. The two men glared at each other. Surely they weren't going to snipe at each other again.

"Now, before anything starts between you two, I remind you . . ."

Neeskah cut her off. He stood by the hogan. "Carter. You come 'ere."

John hesitated as if reviewing mentally the process for standing up with such stiff limbs. Slowly he collected his legs beneath him and rose. He followed Neeskah to the base of the cliff beyond the mesquites. Dasanie was already there, staring up at the rocks. He pointed. Excitedly, John stretched out his arm, waving and pointing. He dropped to his knees and clawed through the talus at the base of the rocks. Talking rapidly and nodding, he held up a bit of something for Neeskah's inspection. He smashed the bit between two stones, stood up and discussed the crumbs.

Linc scowled. "Now what's all that?"

"Hopeful. Very hopeful. Look at him! His enthusiasm speaks to Dasanie more than words could that fossils are indeed the quarry. The dull nickel may well be picking up some luster."

"Whatever that means. Wish they'd go just a little farther. I'd break for it. Prob'ly get away clean."

"Shall I create some sort of diversion?" Naomi wanted to help.

"Too late. Here they come back."

John was glowing, as if these mesquites were Christmas trees full of gifts.

Dasanie pointed to Naomi. "You read and write good?"

162

"I should hope so."

"Me and her." Dasanie was staring at her, but it wasn't his leer.

"Why not I take her?" Neeskah sounded suspicious.

"These two might be stronger'n me, but they can't handle you."

"I guess then. But you listen. You aren't back quick, I leave these two unburied and come get you. And I find you; don't think I won't."

Naomi looked at John. "What's happening?"

John rubbed his hands together. "That bedding layer promises to be everything I came to Arizona to find! It could be the dig of the century. Neeskah and Dasanie realize it's worth a very good price, so you and Dasanie will go down to Flagstaff and . . ."

"No." Neeskah scowled. "Pipe Spring. It's farther but not much people. Safer."

"Very well, Pipe Spring. Deseret Telegraph. You'll send a telegram to New Haven in my name requesting additional funds."

"Ransom."

"In a way. More a payment for goods. Dr. Marsh will pay, and it's well worth it."

"And you two stay here with Neeskah and these people to ensure my cooperation."

"Dasanie seems to think you're more manageable; less likely to bolt. I trust I needn't remind you that if you two don't accomplish your task on schedule, Neeskah will kill both of us."

"I rather guessed as much. I'll do my best." Naomi watched tiny blue flames swim about on the coals. There stood John above her and here sat Linc beside her. She could feel Linc's presence, but she could not feel John's. Strange.

John was talking to Dasanie, but his eyes were on the cliff. "I suggest that two thousand is about the maximum they'll send without delay or fuss. Now there's a problem. I doubt there's two thousand cash anywhere around Pipe Spring. Flag yes, but not Pipe Spring."

Dasanie grunted. "How many days it take?"

"Probably four or five, perhaps even a week until you have the money in your hand."

Neeskah wagged his head. "You go to Pipe Spring. You send 'em to give us the money in Flag. Then you come right back here. Don' wait around with her up there. Come here. Then we all go to Flag and collect. And you bring me a copy of the telegram."

John nodded. "That would protect you. You're clever, Neeskah. I sensed that when I hired you. Too bad I didn't notice the larcenous streak."

Neeskah frowned. "What zhat mean?"

"A tendency to a life of crime," Naomi translated. "You are a crook and a scoundrel, Neeskah." She could say such things whereas John or Linc could not—not safely.

The Indian laughed. "Eh! Tha's right! And a thousand bucks richer soon. Live a long time on that kinda money. Live real good." Something struck him funny and he laughed all the harder. He picked up two bridles and wandered off, still chuckling.

Linc, now the camp cook, mixed some cornmeal gruel for breakfast. Naomi could not say how it tasted five minutes after she ate it. She watched absently as Linc helped saddle Dasanie's bay and his own Nizhoni. She hardly heard when Neeskah ordered her up on her horse. Like a creaky old woman, she climbed aboard Nizhoni. Dasanie kept her reins. Again she would be led about as if she were a load on a pack mule.

They crossed the grassy meadow and descended into the

164

canyon long before the sun could thread its shining fingers down between the walls. Naomi had noted that horses are uphill creatures. They rake and lunge their way up hills much easier than they can stumble downhill. She was lurched and shaken; she gripped the saddle horn with both hands.

She remembered the sky as being blue when they entered the canyon. It was white when they emerged. As they wound through the faceless hills, the overcast grew thicker, the air heavier. The lightest part of the sullen sky hung directly before them. Dasanie was leading her south.

She spoke up. "Pipe Spring is north. Where are you going?"

"Neeskah's worried you get away from me. You won't. Not with all your lovers waiting back there. Flagstaff's closer."

"I see. Also, Pipe Spring is a Mormon settlement and perhaps you'd like a beer or two."

Dasanie snickered.

"And then, the time we don't spend on the road you can spend waiting for the money. About the time Neeskah expects us back, you'll be leaving Flagstaff alone with two thousand dollars. You have no intention of going back to that box canyon."

"Maybe. Maybe not. You don' know and you can't afford to guess. Can't risk your precious lovers."

"And please stop calling them my lovers." She sat frustrated. She took scant comfort in the fact that riding was no longer such a painful experience. She rocked along with her horse's gait and applied her mind to the immediate peril. She could see no way to force Dasanie to return to that canyon, with or without any money. Yet there must be some way.

The dingy sky grew thicker. A chill wind picked up. The

air pushed sluggishly past them, also headed southward. Surely it wouldn't snow again! Linc had as much as promised.

They were approaching a north-south road of sorts. To the far south she saw half a dozen wagons inching northward like a canvas-arched, disjointed caterpillar. Dasanie emerged onto the road and kneed his horse south. The wagons grew slowly larger.

Naomi counted seven wagons and five or six ragged flocks of sheep and goats. They were Navajo, all Navajo. Was it a whole clan on the march? Apparently. The wagons seemed heavily laden. They were accompanied by a dozen riders, most of them half-grown children. Naomi had hoped there would be at least one Anglo there, someone to signal, with whom to seek refuge. She sighed.

Dasanie spoke to the lead wagon as they approached. The driver responded. Again Naomi felt like some sort of trophy paraded past these Indians. She looked at the stony faces with her own stony countenance.

The seventh wagon dawdled thirty feet to the rear. Naomi almost gasped aloud; Doli and Kee sat in the wagon box! Doli had mounted the iron hoops and canvas on her wagon, but it was still the wagon in which Naomi had once ridden. Naomi felt a happy little rush of recognition. Kee's arm was cradled in a sling much cleaner than Dasanie's. Dasanie said something to him and he ducked behind his mother's arm, bashful.

Doli stared at Naomi, stared at Nizhoni, then stared at Naomi again. When Dasanie spoke to her, she answered almost absently. Behind Dasanie's back Naomi stabbed a finger at Nizhoni and then drew the finger quickly across her throat. How universal was that gesture? Did Doli understand? Did she recognize Naomi? Even if she did not (all Anglo women probably looked alike to her), she surely knew Nizhoni.

And now the wagons were past. They creaked and clunked on up the road. An ewe must have been separated from a lamb; there was a flurry of anxious bleating. The sounds receded further and further. Naomi dared not look back.

Dasanie twisted in his saddle. "That woman. She took her time staring."

"I don't blame her. Nizhoni is a lovely animal. When you spoke and she answered, were you offering to sell him?"

"Woulda sold him if she asked. Do you good to walk."

From the wagons behind them, a voice called. Dasanie stopped and craned his neck. With an excuse at last, Naomi twisted around to look.

The whole caravan had stopped in the road. The driver of the wagon just ahead of Doli's was standing beside his rig. He waved an arm and called out in Navajo, separating the syllables to make up for the distance.

Dasanie wrenched his bay around and thumped his heels in its ribs. "Maybe you gonna walk after all."

Naomi's breastbone fluttered. Perhaps Doli told them about Nizhoni. Even if she did not, here was another opportunity for Naomi to signal them somehow. Ah, but no. These were of the same tribe as Dasanie. They would never take her word against his, and if none of them spoke English, they would not know her words. Perhaps . . . but what use was speculation? She must wait and watch carefully and be alert to any opportunity.

Dasanie rode in beside the wagons and spoke to the driver. He dismounted. He and the other fellow seemed to be discussing Nizhoni. They were both looking him over.

Dasanie caught her eye. "Get off."

Naomi slid to the ground. Nervous, Nizhoni shouldered into her.

167

Doli spoke and the driver picked up Nizhoni's near hind foot. He studied it a moment, nodded and let it down. Three other men were gathering here now. Naomi felt very small and swamped.

The aged Indian from the lead wagon joined them. He spoke only one syllable but Joe Dasanie's face turned instantly hard and wooden. He turned and scowled at her as if she were responsible. She had no idea what she might be responsible for. One of the young drivers slipped Dasanie's knife out of its sheath. Two others muttered together.

Naomi's frustration boiled past containment. She exploded, "What's happening?! Doli, can't you speak any English at all? Kee? Linc's helping you with school. Is Nizhoni's foot hurt? Why did he do that just now?"

The aged Indian grabbed her arm and led her roughly over to Doli's wagon. "Now you tell us. The horse. Doli say, 'Look at a mark. A scar.' It was there, the mark."

"Doli knows the horse and his owner. The horse is Nizhoni and the owner is Linc . . . I forget his Navajo name, the name his mother gave him. Doli? Linc . . . ?"

"Naguey." Kee answered. So he knew some English.

"Yes! This man is Joe Dasanie. He and a partner named Neeskah are part of a group." She looked from face to face. "Linc told me about raiders, left over from the old days. Men who still rob and kill, who never quit raiding after the Long Walk. Dasanie and Neeskah are two of them. They . . ."

Kee burst out in Navajo and the aged Indian silenced him. Naomi took that as a sign to continue, even though Dasanie was speaking in protest behind her.

"Naguey and an Anglo named John Carter are captives in their camp. Dasanie here is taking me to Flagstaff to demand ransom money from the man John Carter works for. I think Dasanie does not mean to go back to their camp. I think he means to take all the money for himself. If he does that, his friends will kill John and Naguey." She stopped to listen to her own story with their ears. Who would ever believe such seemingly blatant fiction?

Dasanie seemed to be having his say and then some. The old man listened and watched and said nothing. Naomi much preferred instant action and nothing decisive seemed to be happening. When the old man spoke, all other argument ceased. He asked a question and Dasanie answered. He asked another. Dasanie answered. The old man shook his head; apparently that was the wrong answer. Dasanie began to look frightened.

The old man turned to Naomi. "This man says he took the Long Walk, but he answers my questions wrong. He was not there."

"You mean when the army drove the Dineh from Arizona to New Mexico during the war?"

"The army was going to send us to Oklahoma with many other nations. This man does not know why the army sent us back here instead. Everyone on the Long Walk knows that."

"I see!" Naomi felt the barest glimmer of hope. "The army never did round up the real trouble-makers, the raiders, because they were hiding out. It helps prove he was a marauder."

The man frowned. Apparently *marauder* was not in his vocabulary. "Maybe your story is true. Naguey, other, not dead yet?"

"Not when we left this morning."

"Where? Where is this camp?"

"I don't know, I'm sorry. It's a tiny narrow canyon which opens up into a box canyon—actually, a box valley, a huge meadow surrounded by cliffs. I'm not sure I could find my way back there."

"You came straight here?"

"Yes. From there to here. We left there this morning."

The man turned to one of the young men and rattled off some terse instructions. The man nodded, spoke to another and trotted away up the road on foot. Naomi watched them a moment.

Doli and Kee joined in the general barrage of Navajo that swirled around Naomi's ears. Doli would have a special score to settle with these brigands if they really were the raiders. Indeed, all these Indians would. They were migrating to avoid the consequences these particular outlaws might bring upon all Navajos. Perhaps others in this party knew grief first-hand because of Dasanie's proud raiders.

Dasanie's hand whipped out unexpectedly. He grabbed Naomi's arm and flung her into the tight little knot of men. He swung up onto his horse and yelled. The horse leaped forward, wild-eyed . . . and smashed into the horses ridden by two little girls. Dasanie's bay staggered, fell to its knees and lurched back to its feet. Dasanie shifted and tried to hang on with his good arm. He could not. He hung suspended a moment between heaven and earth, then slid casually off into the dirt at the old man's feet. The two little girls were grinning.

The old Indian had not moved an inch. He was looking at Dasanie, but was speaking in English—to Naomi. "We go look. See what you say. Two men now following tracks, where you came from. Maybe this is true. Maybe we will find the men who would drive us away from our homes with their evil. Doli say Naguey help her many times. Maybe this time we help him. Maybe."

CHAPTER 19

NAOMI ONCE SAW A murderer back in Ohio when she was very small. Her family was returning home from Toledo one evening following the river road. A black moriah passed them on its way to town. A bulky, ponderous black box, the prison wagon had only one window, a little barred hole in its back door. That single window framed a man's sallow face as he peered out at the freedom he had forfeited. She never knew whom he had killed nor when he met his end. She remembered only that stark and stricken, lonely face. That murderer had frightened her then.

Dasanie frightened her now, but not in the same way. Yet he was the same sort of criminal. He rode in the back of the lead wagon and stared morosely at the short little rifle the driver of the second wagon cradled in his lap. Dasanie's horse, and Naomi's, were tied behind Doli's wagon and Naomi again rode in that wagon seat. Doli drove and Kee scrunched between the women.

The language barrier aside, apparently no one had anything to talk about. The springs creaked, the horses plodded and occasionally sneezed or snorted, the wagon rattled, the harness murmured in gentle little noises. The people said nothing.

The sky was thickening again, ever darker. Snow? It was nearly cold enough. Naomi's cheeks could feel the nip. She glanced down at Kee, huddled as close to his mother as possible. Impulsively, she opened her woolen cape and dragged it around behind him, tucking him in close to her. He stiffened a few moments, uncertain, then seemed to decide this was all right. Her fingers brushed his hands; they were very cold.

She spoke distinctly. "How does your arm feel? Are you doing well?"

He smiled and muttered, "Good" in a small bashful voice.

The wagons ahead stopped. The old man hauled his team aside and they left the road. Was this where Dasanie had joined the road? Naomi couldn't tell. There was Dasanie with his feet dangling off the back. There was the young man in the second wagon. The remaining wagons followed in line; the caterpillar turned the corner effortlessly. Naomi smiled in pure admiration for these people's flexibility. Here they were on the way north when this problem dropped upon them, a bolt from the blue. And now they were headed in a new direction, with a *belagana* and one of their own who might or might not be a dangerous brigand. Yet they acted as though this were a normal, uneventful day.

Could they find that tiny slit in the rock face, that narrow defile? Naomi probably could not. Dasanie would certainly be no help.

Scattered splashes of white came drifting down out of the sodden sky. Not again! Eons ago she sat on Dasanie's bay horse outside Linc's hogan and admired the crisp purity of

172

snow. "Last snow of the season" Linc called it. He had promised.

She thought about the very first occasion when she perched huddled in his arms and the snow dropped out of the darkness to touch her. She had mentioned something then about the frying pan and the fire.

Well, she was still there, poised between them. But now John and Linc were there too. She prayed that God's protective hand would extend to them.

Now it was all she could do to stay in the wagon seat. The road had been rutted enough, but this cross-country travel pitched the wagons about dreadfully. Naomi tried to see what lay ahead and could not. They followed the sixth wagon and hoped it was negotiating the best route possible.

They seemed to lurch along for years but it was only hours. When the wagon ahead eventually stopped, Naomi sighed with relief. Her whole body felt jiggly. The woman in the sixth wagon stood up and called across the canvas to Doli who nodded and drove her team up beside theirs. She climbed out and disappeared around back. Apparently they were to camp here. Good. Because of the overcast the sun was setting early tonight, and the snow was still falling thickly.

Naomi felt utterly alien. She looked at Kee. Kee studied the floor of the wagon. Naomi stood up and stretched. She climbed down over the wheel. She'd help with unharnessing, but she had no idea how to go about it. Doli and Kee must camp pretty much without her help. She felt both alien and ignorant.

Kee struck out, seeking wood. Naomi could help with that simple task. She more or less followed Kee about, lest she become lost and separated in this monotonous countryside. She was amazed how much a nine-year-old knew about fuels. He ignored combustible-looking things and

173

picked up others. He ripped out this bush but not that seemingly identical one beside it.

Linc knew all that sort of thing. She remembered vaguely the bulky blob of brush he had plopped on the fire under the overhang, and how the flames had flared up. She thought about his face in the orange fireglow that night, about his worried frown as he watched her. His Anglo half cared about this Anglo woman in distress, even as his Indian half knew exactly what to do. How could she have been impatient with God for providing Linc Rawlins when she needed him? No one else would have served as well. Such ingratitude! When she and Kee returned to the wagon, Doli was already preparing the batter for corncakes.

If Naomi was ignorant about camping, she did take comfort in one area of expertise. She sat down on a rock near the incipient fire as snowflakes floated by. "Kee, Naguey says you're learning to read and write."

Again the big dark eyes were downcast. He nodded.

"Learning interests me very much. I'm a teacher. Will you show me what you're doing?"

He considered her request a moment. Suddenly he hopped up, jogged to the back of the wagon, and clambered inside. Naomi heard clunks and riffling. Doli called and seemed content with Kee's reply. She glanced over at Naomi and went back to her cooking.

Kee jumped out onto the ground and brought Naomi a thickly loaded bookstrap. He handed the whole bundle to her and sat down shyly on the rock beside her.

She unbuckled the strap and shuffled through the books and papers, absolutely amazed. "And Naguey is your teacher?"

He nodded.

The Webster speller was ragged and battered. It was the 1857 Merriam edition, so quite possibly it had been Linc's

174

as a child, and perhaps some child's before him. But the reader—McGuffey's Third Eclectic—had come to Kee's hands brand-new. "Where are you in your reader, Kee?"

He opened it to pages 80/81 and handed it back to her.

She smiled at the familiar line cut of a pasha and his elephant on page 80. "Have you ever seen a real elephant?"

He shook his head.

"Did Naguey describe elephants to you?"

"Real big, he says." Kee's voice was barely audible.

"Oh my, yes! Huge!" Naomi jumped up and stood on her rock, stretching her arm as high as possible. "It's back would be this far off the ground or even higher. And an elephant is wide. Massive. Its sheer size makes it just a bit frightening. Men ride on elephants. How do you suppose they get up there?"

Kee frowned. "Stirrups?"

She held her other hand at nose level. "The stirrups would only reach down to here."

"A rope?"

"Do you see a rope in that picture?"

Kee picked up his reader and pored over the picture.

Naomi sat down again. "Imagine that elephant getting down on its front knees. He curls his trunk—his nose—up so. Then the man who rides him—the man is called a mahout—climbs up the front of the elephant, up its head and face, and straddles him on the neck just behind his ears. The elephant stands up, and his rider guides him by kicking him behind his ears, with his toes."

Kee stared at the picture. He stared at her. "Really?"

"Really. A circus came through Maumee many years ago and father took us. The elephant man told father how it was done, and I was listening."

"No elephants around here."

"No elephants in America at all, except the ones in circuses. This picture is of an elephant in some faraway country in Asia. You see, all the men dress differently there. Turbans, loose pantaloons.''

"Not Anglos?"

"Not Anglos."

Kee looked her in the eye for the first time that day. Suddenly he leafed madly through his reader. He held up another page. "What's this?"

"It's a picture of waves on the seacoast. The ocean. Did you try to read it?"

"Sorta. I didn't understand."

"And no wonder. It is a narrative of little waves on the shore talking about their mother, the sea." She read the piece. That necessitated describing the ocean and the waves lapping (none of which she had ever seen, but she was quite familiar with Lake Erie, which she substituted). This in turn invited comparison with the endless desert and sky. The lesson lasted nearly half an hour. By then Doli had nearly finished preparations for the evening meal. Naomi was grateful for the lesson not only because it got her mind off her dilemma, but also because it made her feel a bit useful.

Doli never did formally invite Naomi to eat with them. She simply assumed the extra mouth to feed. Naomi sat beside Kee and ate everything that was offered her. These irregular meals made her uncharacteristically and impolitely ravenous.

It was dark when the meal was finished. Proud as royalty, Kee trotted out his yellow copybook and demonstrated his writing prowess. He read his current lesson to her and did simple multiplications in his head. Linc had taught him very well. Naomi watched him trace the written words and recalled stories of Abraham Lincoln reading by firelight. She spent much idle thought mulling over the subtle parallels and ramifications.

Wrapped in her blanket, Doli spoke suddenly from across the fire.

Kee strapped his books back together and glanced up at Naomi, somewhat ashamed. "Ma asks if you wanna marry Naguey."

Naomi stared at Doli and Doli stared back, totally unabashed. Naomi shook her head. "No. Remember I mentioned a man with him? An Anglo named John? I'm considering marrying John, not Naguey."

Kee translated and Doli spoke. Kee winced. "You love him?"

"Love John? Why yes, I suppose so." Now why did she make such a spineless answer to a strong and direct question? Of course she loved John. John was perfect for her in every way, wasn't he?

Kee looked disappointed. "You don' like Naguey?"

"Oh, I like him very much. As a friend. He helped me when I needed help. And he's very gentle and smart and kind. And he's a marvelous teacher, I see. I admire that. But admiring and marrying are two very different things."

Kee's head snapped around and Naomi followed his eyes. The old man stepped silently out of the snowy darkness and hunkered down beside Doli's fire.

"The scouts came back. They went to the canyon. You speak truth. They found Naguey's trail to the top. It is as you say. Tomorrow we look some more—we think."

"That's all? Look and think?" She bit her lip. "I'm sorry. Of course you must look and think. Those men are wily and dangerous. They've been outlaws a long time."

The old man nodded toward Kee. "You like him."

"He's a charming boy. And clever. Very smart. I'm a schoolteacher. I wish all my pupils could be like him."

The man nodded and stared at the fire. What should Naomi say? She waited. He studied the fire for long minutes. "We talk about some things, scouts and me. Maybe we use you. You're strong woman. Tough. You help?"

"Yes, of course, any way I can." Naomi frowned, puzzled. He called her tough and strong, and the way he said it made it sound complimentary, as if toughness and strength were virtues in a lady. How inside-out this culture was, to expect such traits in its women! Did Linc also consider her tough?

Doli was certainly tough and strong; she could not have made her way this long otherwise. Moreover she knew exactly how to balance herself between leaning upon a man and being self-sufficient. Tough and strong, yet vulnerable, she was the perfect wife for a man in this culture, and capable, dependable Linc was the perfect man for her. He claimed he didn't love her, not really. Naomi didn't believe him. After all Doli was perfect for him in every way.

. . . Just as John was perfect for Naomi.

CHAPTER 20

BACK EAST, BAD WEATHER dawdled for days on end. Here in the desert rain and snow might fall, but the clouds, having done their service, usually departed promptly. Naomi rather liked the arrangement better. The evening sky was still hazy but the thick overcast had gone; blue tinged the milky white. Of all the snow that had fallen yesterday and last night, only the barest skiff remained in the tiny nooks of permanent shade.

She sat in Nizhoni's saddle at the mouth of that narrow defile. Impatient, the horse tossed his head and pivoted a tight little circle, as nervous as she. Patches on his shoulders and flanks were sweaty dark. Good. That would lend credence to her story. She watched in the far distance. She must not be hasty.

Somewhere in the hills out there, the seven wagons sat. The women and children waited there and so did Joe Dasanie, bound hand and foot. She had no idea where the men had gone, for she could not understand their gestures, let alone their words. In her prayers this evening she had to

179

lean entirely on the Holy Spirit's help, for she had no glimpse of the overall plan. She knew only her own part, and it made her uneasy. If something should go wrong, and she could not play her given part, how would she know what to do instead?

The haze was dissipating. Unveiled, the sun broke forth for a few glorious moments before it plunged behind the western horizon. It was time. She urged Nizhoni into the defile, up the winding trail now familiar to him. He knew green grass awaited him. Did he also remember Linc was there?

She stopped by the boulder pile, but no one peeked out. She called out anyway. "You know me. I'm returning."

No response.

They scrambled up the final dry rockfall, rounded the final bend, and stepped out into the open valley. The dusky sky spread an even glow across the meadow. No fires burned, no lights showed. She saw no human being at all. At the far end the horses paused from cropping grass to lift their heads as one—looking not at Naomi, of course, but at Nizhoni. John's horse whinnied. She rode at a walk to the head of the valley, listening to the silence.

"You back too soon!" Neeskah stood directly behind her, that ugly pistol grown fast to his hand. She slid to the ground and pulled a yellow paper out of her sleeve. Nizhoni threw his head up and jerked the reins from her hands. He cantered across the wash to join his friends.

She handed the paper to Neeskah and hoped he couldn't tell it was a page from a copy tablet. "Dasanie insisted on going to Flagstaff instead. I don't know what he intended to do with me, but I know he doesn't plan to come back here. He'll probably get the money in three or four days, but I don't care. I had to come back."

Neeskah squinted at the paper in the gathering darkness.

Did he know how to read? She had printed it in large block letters and it looked official to the unsophisticated eye:

SPLENDID FIND STOP REQUIRE TWO THOUSAND
DOLLARS TO SECURE OWNERSHIP STOP PLEASE
SEND IMMEDIATELY STOP ENTHUSIASTICALLY JOHN
HARRISON CARTER

"How you get away?"

"Some people helped me."

Neeskah glared. "I don' believe you."

"I really don't care. Where are John and Linc?"

Neeskah grinned, mirthless. "Big Heart Lady. Joe says you got angels. They take care of you. He's afraid of your angels. I'm not. We go to Flag, get the money. You and me. Go saddle my horse. Quick!"

"Where are John and Linc?!"

"Go!"

The old Navajo had told her to find some cause to get away from Neeskah and find Naguey. He had just given her opportunity to leave; she must not stand arguing. She picked up Neeskah's bridle and walked out across the sparse and wavy grass. Snow showed as a bluish glow in the close shadows against the cliffs, but the grass was only icy wet.

For the first time in this whole fearful business, Naomi felt pure, gripping, forbidding terror. It robbed her strength and trammeled her breath. It bound her mind and body as with wire; she could neither move easily nor think. She didn't fear for herself; women were seldom murdered outright. But Linc was a dangerous antagonist, and John's usefulness was at an end. Had Neeskah buried them already under a pile of stones? She found herself looking about anxiously for fresh dirt or stacked rocks. The horses watched her approach a few moments and began to stroll away.

A familiar voice shouted behind her. She wheeled. Dasanie came running on foot out of the opening of the defile! Dasanie! How had he escaped? How could he . . . ? Futile questions now—here he was, and now Neeskah and the others would know she was lying. Worse, whatever those Navajos planned would no longer be a surprise. From nowhere, half a dozen men appeared.

Before she could think, a rifle blasted. The shot echoed from wall to wall; she could not tell from whence it came. Trailing a glowing tail across the twilight sky, a shooting star whistled down from the top of the cliff. The flame slammed into Neeskah's brush hogan. Neeskah wheeled, staring. Flames licked eagerly at the dry branches. More fiery arrows flashed from sky to earth. Some of them struck only wet grass and died a-smoldering. Others splacked into the brushy hogans and mesquite thickets. Last year's grass roared into flame.

Up on the rim, shadowy silhouettes pushed flaming brush over the side. Cascades of sparks and flame crashed down into the mesquite thickets. Smoke was rapidly filling this rock-strangled valley.

From the far side of the valley, someone screamed. One of the old marauders came running out of his burning hogan, a man on fire. He threw himself into the wet grass, shrieking; Naomi lost sight of him.

Neeskah had forgotten her. She dropped the bridle, grabbed two handfuls of skirts, and ran for Neeskah's burning hogan. The doorway was afire. She ran back and began yanking at poles and brush. The hogan wall rattled. She pulled harder, loosening a vertical support. She realized she was yelling Linc's name. She had better call to John also.

The factions were shooting it out in earnest now. Every gunshot multiplied itself in reverberations off the canyon walls. The Battle of Gettysburg could not have been this loud.

The hogan rattled again and bulged suddenly outward. Someone was battering it from inside. She heard a muffled "One two three!" The wall bulged out again; she grabbed what ought to be the weakest part and pulled backward—pulled, pulled. A dry pole cracked and gave. She fell backward into the wet ground. Like a cork from a champagne bottle, John popped out of the ruptured wall. He writhed in the grass, serpentine-like; Naomi realized his hands and feet were tied and he was trying to roll away from the hogan.

The burning roof cracked and roared; the hogan caved in. Linc was in the broken wall, and now Naomi was pulling on him. He tumbled against her and they rolled together into the frosty grass. Linc's coat was smoking. Naomi was crying. Why should she be crying now?

John was on his knees, watching the inferno. His head wagged, incredulous. "Seconds ago I was inside that conflagration!"

Naomi plucked ineffectually at the ropes around Linc's wrists. "I don't have a . . . a knife . . ." The tears streamed down her cheeks. But she did have teeth. She picked at the knot as if it were a tangle in a skein of knitting wool. The knot was loosening.

"Where'd you find all the help?" Why did Linc expect her to talk with her teeth full?

"It's Navajos. That clan moving north."

He squirmed and twisted and his arms were free. He worked at the cords around his ankles. "Doli with 'em?"

"Yes. And Kee."

"Where's Dasanie?"

"I don't know. He's here somewhere."

"Give John a hand there. And keep your head down!"

"Don't go . . ."

183

But Linc bolted to his feet and started forward. Instantly he came flying back against her. He knocked her backward and they slammed together into John. Naomi struggled, flattened within an octopus of churning arms and legs.

Linc's weight rolled aside, and a strong arm yanked Naomi to her feet. It spun her around and clamped around her neck. A burning brand waved close beside her eye and cheek. That panic surged over her again.

A voice rasped beside her ear, "You two don' move or I burn her eyes out." Dasanie!

He had abandoned the sling. His good arm wrapped securely around her neck and the other brandished a burning stick.

"How did you get free of Doli; the women had you?" She could barely speak with the crook of his arm pinching her neck.

"They don' have angels. Now your angels don' do you no good no more. And 'specially his angels." The head beside hers nodded toward Linc.

"Why did you come back?" She didn't care, but she wanted to keep him talking.

Linc twisted to put his feet under him. Dasanie gave Naomi a disciplinary little shake, and Linc quit moving. He watched Dasanie as a cat watches a mouse, waiting.

John watched as intently, though he could do nothing with his wrists and ankles bound. "You'll never leave here alive unless you give yourself over to us. Be sensible, man!"

"He's right." Naomi tried to ease the pressure on her throat by twisting. "Why didn't you just keep running? You'd be safe somewhere by now."

"I come to warn my friends. Tell 'em about you. But too late. You take my pride and now you take my friends. You'll pay. You all gonna pay."

In one split-second motion, Linc flicked from sitting to crouching, ready to pounce. "Your friends are done here and Carter's not worth the trouble. Your fight's with me now, Dasanie. Come and get me."

Dasanie clamped tighter. Naomi could no longer breathe. Dasanie grunted. "No. First you watch your ladylove get blind. Then I take you!"

The burning stick flashed toward Naomi's face which she tried to protect with her hands. When the torch flared past her cheek, she smelled hair burning. Linc came slamming in. He and Dasanie fought over the torch with Naomi in the middle. Dasanie locked her head tightly against him, using her for a shield. He stabbed at her again with the stick. Suddenly she was flung free.

She fell, face first and skidding, into the cold wet grass. Had he ignited her hair? She squirmed in the grass, rubbing her whole head in it. She thought briefly of the way Nizhoni looked as he rolled in the sandy wash. Her head thoroughly soaked, she wrenched around to a sitting position.

John was calling to her. She wanted to go to him and help him with the ropes around his wrists, but her legs were fluid. They lay beneath her in a helpless puddle.

Linc and Dasanie tussled and flailed, black shadows against a dancing yellow backdrop. They teetered, straining against each other, then fell together through the flaming curtain. They disappeared behind it in a blast of sparks. Naomi shrieked.

Dasanie was on his feet instantly. He ran out into the open meadow. The back of his shirt smoldered and burst into flame. From beyond the fiery curtain Linc hurtled after him. With a flying leap he wrapped around Dasanie's waist and dragged the man down. They rolled and wrestled in the grass; the gangling legs kicked wildly.

Two men came running this way across the meadow.

They both carried rifles of some sort. Were they friend or foe?

Naomi lurched to her feet. Her knees buckled, so she tried again. Now she was running toward John. If those two men were outlaws, Linc would need help; he would need John. She plopped down beside John simply by letting her legs collapse.

He thrust his arms toward her. "Here. I made a little headway with it, I think. Were you burned?"

She shook her head numbly. Her fingers seemed to be accomplishing nothing, and yet the cords were loosening.

"Ha!" He ripped one hand free, though the cord scuffed half the skin off his wrist. They turned their efforts to the ropes on his ankles but Naomi seemed to be getting in his way. She twisted to her knees. Where was Linc?

Linc was standing surrounded by brilliance, his legs braced squarely. He hauled Dasanie to his feet only to flatten him again with a wide-swinging punch. Those two men were just now reaching him. John clambered to his feet.

"Hurry!" Naomi seized his arm and started toward Linc. She toyed with the idea of snatching up a burning stick. But despite the roaring flames, she saw no likely weapons. John seemed to be spoiling for a fight, but when they reached the others the fight was over. One of the two gun-wielding Navajos was the old man. Friends.

Naomi would have asked Linc an utterly stupid, useless question ("Are you on fire?") and then felt foolish, but mercifully she was too shaken, too winded to speak. She wanted so much to cling to Linc's arm but she remembered that John was her choice, not he. She laid her hand on John's arm. He wrapped around her and drew her in close.

The valley and its walls showed up bright as day in the light of a hundred leaping fires. Glowing yellow, a dense pall of smoke hung like a ceiling from rim to rim. The fires had banished winter. The valley was as hot as a summer afternoon. Naomi's eyes burned and watered.

She lay her head on John's shoulder. "It was all so chaotic. Do you suppose Neeskah was . . . I mean, do you think he's still alive?"

Linc must have swallowed a lot of smoke. He hacked and coughed and tried to catch up on his breathing. He looked at the old man. "We lose anybody?"

"Don' know. Maybe."

In the smoky glow beyond the wash, a hooting voice shouted something which sounded derisive. Neeskah was alive, all right. He had caught Nizhoni and was securely in the saddle. Twisting Nizhoni's head toward the defile, he slammed his heels in the horse's ribs. Nizhoni lunged away down the wash at a dead run.

Naomi moaned. There went poor Linc's horse again, and scant hope it would be recovered this time! By the time Linc caught another horse to give chase, Neeskah would be long gone. Even if a Navajo were guarding the canyon, he would recognize Nizhoni as a friend and realize too late he was being ridden by an enemy.

Neeskah was escaping scot-free, and Linc would never reclaim his horse.

CHAPTER 21

IN 1812, RUSSIANS BURNED their beloved Moscow rather than let Napoleon have her. During the war, southerners in the path of a northern army would kill livestock and pets and let them rot lest the abominable Yankees make use of them. Solomon threatened to slice a baby in two and give half to each squabbling woman who claimed it. Naomi remembered her history at the oddest moments.

Now, she saw, the old Navajo was swinging his rifle up to his shoulder. Neeskah was riding low, and the smoke obscured vision; the man was aiming for the horse to prevent Neeskah's escape.

"No!" Linc's hand shot out and pushed the rifle barrel down. He whistled, that shrill, warbling whistle he had once called Nizhoni's come-here whistle.

Nizhoni skidded to a stop and wheeled. Neeskah wrenched his head around again toward the canyon defile. Nizhoni shook his tousled head and waltzed in tight little circles. The piercing whistle beckoned again. Nizhoni reared high and lunged forward. Naomi had seen him do that before but never so violently. He tucked the gray head between his front legs and crowhopped. He leaped higher and ducked, swapping ends in midair. Neeskah was no match for the determined horse. He came loose, lifted gracefully away from the saddle, and slammed into the ground. Like a knight victorious, Nizhoni came trotting to Linc, his nose and tail high.

Linc walked out to meet him. The gray head buried itself in Linc's chest, pushed against the soiled sheepskin coat. Linc spent long minutes just rubbing Nizhoni's chin and neck and ears. Perhaps not all the tears in Naomi's eyes came from the smoke.

She looked over at the old Navajo. "You didn't have to believe me. You didn't have to risk so much just to save Linc—Naguey. And John. I'm very grateful."

He shook his head. "Maybe we do this, maybe not. We didn't know. Then I watched you read with Kee. You're Anglo, but you care about Dineh. What you did with Kee, that said many things about you. We want to help. Then we say, this Dasanie turn against Carter and you. Pretty soon he turns against other Anglos. Then all the Anglos come kill us. All Indians look alike to Anglos. Better stop Dasanie, Neeskah, right now."

"Good. Then you get some benefit also. But it seems too much . . . all this . . . The whole valley's burning, it seems. And those men . . ."

A little knot of prisoners sat in the middle of the wash. The victors stood about, guns cradled casually in their arms, as if nothing untoward had happened this night. How many had died? Naomi didn't want to think about it.

"Now it is very good. These men made it very bad for Dineh. Maybe make things bad for Anglos and that's bad for Dineh. No one in my clan wanted to go north, but it was

189

best. Now these men are ours. No more trouble. I think now we go back home. It's good.''

Naomi looked at the scoundrel lying at her feet. He hardly appeared to be trouble now. He was staring at her. He said something to the old man.

The Navajo cocked his head. "He wants you go away. He's afraid of your angels. Says they are too powerful for the spirits he called.''

"Of course. My God is more powerful than all his spirits put together.'' Naomi looked Dasanie right in the eye, and pretended she had never doubted her Lord's ability to deliver.

"Religion again!'' John laughed and squeezed her shoulder affectionately.

She pressed against him, suddenly weak-kneed. "Not as pure as it ought to be, though. I'm afraid my faith faltered more than once.''

"Will you quit worrying so constantly about such things?'' He nuzzled her. "Your faith is just fine. Overdeveloped, if anything.'' He nodded toward the old man. "What do I do about these two ex-employees?''

"Nothing.''

"Come, man! I'll see their heads roll in court, if nothing else.''

"John!'' Naomi grabbed his free hand. "You can't take these two Dineh out of the hands of their people to drag them in front of an Anglo judge. That's exactly what this man does *not* want—contact and trouble with white authorities.''

"Attempted murder, kidnapping, destruction of property, horse theft . . .''

"Their own people have been victims too—not just you. Let them take care of the matter themselves, according to their own laws and customs.''

"But all the trouble they caused. My camera." John looked around at the stony faces. He sighed as the diplomat within took over. "What choice do I have? Let's leave this inferno." He squeezed her hand. They ambled off toward the narrow canyon. "I'll get my horse tomorrow. The saddle and blanket roll are burnt to embers."

A yellow flutter caught the wild firelight. John released her and picked it up out of the wet grass. He studied it, smiling. "A child's copybook. This was your telegram?"

"Blew clear down to this end of the valley. Amazing it didn't burn."

"I assume you never reached a telegraph office."

"Got nowhere near."

"'A splendid find'. So true. I can hardly wait to send word. Why, Dr. Marsh can have a crew in here by June."

"I thought that wording would sound like you."

"Ah." He tossed the paper over his shoulder. "Now that we're on the subject . . ."

"What subject?"

"Knowing each other. Knowing how I'd phrase this message, for example. You remember that night a few centuries ago when we disturbed your rest by arguing? I assume you heard most of our harangue."

"The latter part. The loud part. Yes."

A movement near the mouth of the canyon caught her eye. Doli was standing there, watching, with three or four other women. And midway between Doli and her stood Linc, with Nizhoni at his shoulder. He was watching Naomi.

John stopped and gathered both her hands in his. "I spoke then of courting you. To be honest, it slipped out. I hadn't really thought of it at all until that stupid argument raised my hackles. Well, I've been thinking about it quite a bit since then. You share my interests, most of my recent

191

experiences and adventures, this latest not the least. Your personal preferences and tastes match mine. Your appearance is absolutely charming; you're a very pretty woman. Your strong moral fiber, your very capable wit and common sense (which you've demonstrated amply in this present emergency, I might add); all these, in short, would be reason to court you seriously even without any emotional considerations.''

"You flatter me. I made a choice, also. And . . ."

"But I find myself emotionally drawn to you. Perhaps 'enslaved' is not too inappropriate a word. I didn't realize how deeply I cared for you on an emotional level until I watched you ride away behind Joe Dasanie yesterday. I can't describe the dread I felt, the hollow fear of what he might do to you. Fear for your life. I've never experienced anything close to that sort of concern before.''

"I told you at the time—that night, I mean—that I would choose," Naomi interrupted. "And I've done so." She glanced involuntarily toward Linc. He was gazing at her. For all his size and strength and capability, he seemed so vulnerable standing there. She was suddenly and terribly afraid to hurt him.

John charged ahead. "What I'm trying to make known to you, Naomi my dear, is that I love you.''

Her eyes were burning again. Was it smoke? Probably not. She should be relieved and happy. She had waited for this moment ever since she had made her choice, days ago—or centuries ago, as John so aptly put it. Linc was watching, motionless. Nizhoni tossed his gray head.

John glanced uneasily toward Linc and resumed his speech. "I fully realize a proper lady would never weigh crass material considerations when making a decision of this magnitude, and you are above all a proper lady. I think that virtue endears you to me as much as any you could possess.

But I do remind you that such material considerations are a practical part of any marriage union. And you shall have the very best of everything, I promise you.''

She looked into his glowing eyes. He, too, had taken on a large measure of vulnerability. Beneath the veneer of adulthood, were all men little boys? "I hope you won't think less of me, but I did indeed weigh what you call the practical considerations, and prestige not the least of them. I hope this doesn't sound crass. I don't mind being considered practical, of course . . ." Her eyes flicked toward Linc. He was still there, still watching.

"Another practical consideration, my dear, is children. Our children shall enjoy every advantage. I consider that immensely important."

"Absolutely! So do I! That's why I've chosen . . ."

"And I intend that my children shall have the best. The best nannies, the best schools. There are some excellent boarding schools in this country now, though we may think about sending them to England. You see? We're agreed on every major issue and we share so much. I can't think of a single reason that would hinder marriage, can you?"

Doli and the other women had moved further up into the meadow. They were curious, no doubt; the fire was spectacular even as it abated. Linc was looking at Doli.

Naomi took a deep breath. She must force every particle of her attention back to the situation at hand and forget about Linc Rawlins. "Frankly, John, one issue does bother me, very much. I've touched on it before—your cavalier attitude toward God."

"My religious views are not necessarily identical with yours, but we are both Christian adults—by which I mean that neither of us is a pagan." He glanced pointedly at Linc.

"But the depth of your commitment to the person Jesus Christ. Your confidence in the Holy Word. They worry me.

I suppose 'lip service' is the term that comes to my mind."

"You insult me, Naomi." And indeed his air was one of an insulted man. She regretted speaking. "I apologize for being so forthright, but forthrightness seems to be appropriate to the moment. My family has produced ministers and deacons for over four generations. My great-grandfather contributed liberally to the chapel at Yale and was instrumental in its building. It dates from 1757, you know, and a Carter has worshiped in it nearly every week of its existence."

"I'm sure your family is very respectable, John. I'm sorry you construed my comments as aspersions upon your ancestors. But I'm talking about your personal commitment, not your forefathers'. Our God is awesome and His Word inerrant, but you seem to treat both so lightly, as if you were responsible for your own fortunes. And I don't see . . ."

"Of course I'm responsible for my own fortunes! However, I really can't see any justification for this petty bickering. I fail to share your parochial attitude toward religion, but I understand how you came by it, what with your upbringing and all. I don't expect you to embrace the particulars of my own beliefs right away, but as you come to see . . ."

She missed the last part of what he was saying because Linc stole her attention. He swung aboard Nizhoni. She didn't want him to ride away again the way he had the night he first turned her over to John. Doli was on her way north to join relatives; let well enough alone, Linc. And don't leave. Please don't go yet. She had not yet said good-by or thank you.

He cupped her cheek in his hand and physically turned her face back to his. "In short, Naomi, I insist your reservations about religious matters are without foundation.

194

You've blown the issue all out of proportion. Let us put them aside for the moment, at least."

"That will be difficult for me. If only I could draw some assurance of a firmer commitment from you . . ."

"Of course, dear. Whatever pleases you."

"No, John! I really don't think you understand what I'm trying to say."

He raised her hands to his lips and softly kissed her knuckles. "I refuse to be drawn into a theological discussion in the middle of the night while the world is burning all around our ears. The question of the moment is marriage, and I'm asking you right now to share my life and fortunes. Why, even if I should end up on another of these survey expeditions, think how comfortably you'll fit in. We can even . . . What the . . .?!"

Nizhoni's big gray shoulder nudged against him. He thrust out his arm to fend off the clumsy horse. Linc reached down and grabbed Naomi's arm. Without thinking, she gripped his as she had so often done before. He sat erect in his saddle, dragging her straight up, and tilted back, pulling her up onto the bedroll behind. With one arm twisted behind to anchor her firmly, he kneed Nizhoni off toward the canyon at a rocking-horse canter.

"Linc! Let me down this instant!" She looked behind.

John came running after them, shouting out some very ungentlemanly comments. He stopped, not far from Doli, unable to follow further.

"Stop it! Wait a minute! Let me down!" She would pound her fists on his obstinate back, but she had to cling with both hands for dear life. His coat was permeated with the stink of burnt grass and leather.

They entered the defile and rode instantly from heat to cold darkness. Naomi couldn't see a thing; she only hoped the firelight had not blinded Nizhoni. The horse picked his way down that first rockfall and plopped along complacently at a shuffling pace.

"What about my right to choose? You yourself said I have the right to make my own choices—about travel, or marriage or anything. You said no man could presume to make those decisions for me. Not in so many words, of course, but you said that."

"You did choose. I saw the look in your eyes there. Carter mighta been talking your ear off, but I saw your eyes."

"And you think you can just whisk me away without benefit of clergy to some miserable hogan and . . ."

"Whoa! I told you about my attack of conscience, and my pa's God. I meant it. Still do. Besides I need your help. When we were talking about praying that night—you remember?"

"No. Not exactly."

Linc slowed Nizhoni to a walk. They threaded their way around that boulder pile. It was deserted here. "About prayer and church. You see there's this little church in Kansas that didn't think Ma and I were good enough for 'em. I let that one little church sour me on God. Know what I mean?"

"I want to understand."

"I put religion in a church and left it there. You put religion inside yourself. You deal with God—you and Him together. I don't know how to do that and I need you to help me. Because of that one nasty experience, I been keeping my back turned to God, and it's high time I turned around. You know the Bible and praying and all that. I need you."

"Oh. Well, ah, since you put it that way . . ."

"We can get married up at Lee's Ferry on our way north. And I promise you're safe till then. No messing around. Might buy you a horse somewhere around there too."

"But . . ." She didn't know whether to laugh with joy or fly into a rage. The presumptuousness of this unmannered boor . . . ! "I thought you were trying to find your mother."

"I spent two years tracking down rumors. No Tom Oakes, no Mrs. Rawlins, no Biih Yaazh. About time to get on with the rest of my life."

"But what about my right to choose? You said . . ." She stopped because Nizhoni stopped. Impatient, the horse took a few little steps in place.

Linc let go with his arm and twisted in the saddle to meet her eye-to-eye. "You ready to tell me I'm the wrong choice?"

The impudence of this man! She didn't want to hurt him, especially not after all he had done for her, but his behavior was absolutely brazen. He asked, so she would just have to tell him. "It so happens I made my choice days ago, when you two were involved in that ridiculous imbroglio. You remember, that night after I had retired." She looked straight into those delightfully tilted eyes—the better to emphasize her remarks. They were looking straight into hers, melting all over her. The moonshadows in this canyon made them seem even deeper and darker than they were.

She licked her lips nervously. "Understand, the choice was made in the heat of the moment, you might say. I was intensely angry with you two, both of you. Angry to tears. There you were, bickering and squabbling like first-graders when the real enemy was quite possibly prowling the perimeters of camp that very moment. Such choices should always be subject to revision."

It was hardly possible that a man so impertinent and forward would plead with puppy-dog eyes, but he was doing it.

"Please understand the situation from my viewpoint. A

woman must follow her heart, but she must also make practical choices.'' Her eyes left his and drifted down to the darkness by Nizhoni's feet. ''And besides, scooping me up like this is hardly a thoughtful way to invite my attentions.''

''I'm not robbing you of your choice; I already said that. I'm just not giving Carter room to change your mind, that's all.''

''Yes. Well ah . . . but it's so precipitous. And your proposal of marriage—I assume that was it just now—was so . . . so casual . . .''

She would not have dreamed that two persons astride the same horse could kiss effectively. Where there is a will, however, there is a way, and Linc certainly possessed the will. Of course, he was much more comfortable doing anything on horseback than was she. He buried her in a loving, happy swathe of heavy sheepskin, powerful arms, and gentle lips. The kiss made wonderful promises about the years to come.

Stones rattled upcanyon. Perhaps John had corralled and saddled his horse, or perhaps the Navajos were coming out. Linc's arms didn't loosen at all, though he presently lifted away from the kiss.

His face hovered, lingered, above hers. ''Changed my mind.''

Her heart thumped, fearstruck. Was her kiss not responsive enough? Did he have second thoughts about marrying a prim and (quite frankly and honestly) somewhat stuffy spinster?

''Let's get married in Flag instead.'' He was grinning. ''We can have your trunks shipped north. They're probably tripping everybody in the back room of the stage stop. And we can even send John's telegram for him to tell that professor about his boneyard there. Besides,'' the dark eyes sparkled, ''it's a whole lot closer'n Lee's Ferry.'' He

198

released her and twisted straight in his saddle.

Nizhoni lurched into his easy rolling half-jog. He stumbled in the darkness and she wrapped quickly around Linc's waist to avoid slipping.

She laid her head against the broad back. "You heard the saying, 'Marry in haste, repent at leisure'?"

He snorted. "We're not kids, either one of us. We both know what we want, and we don't have a lot of time to waste. I'm ready for this."

"Such words from a confirmed bachelor!" She felt warm and soft. His presence soaked into her, surrounded her, filled her with affection.

"Ain't it something." His voice was lilting, awash with what Naomi could only interpret as plain old joy.

Strong and steady, Nizhoni strode from the dark, cramped canyon out onto the Bajada, from hovering closeness into the broad expanse of desert, from swarming shadows into shimmering moonlight. The snow was gone; no trace of whiteness reflected the silver light anywhere.

The last snow of winter.

She twisted around to look behind. Beyond the scarp to the east, a dull orange cloud hung near the rocks and drifted aloft. Her memory reminded her of the heat and light and loud crackling below that cloud.

Overhead the moon was just starting to come full. Tomorrow night, or the night after, it would lose that last little flat edge. The gray light pulled the distance in close, just as it always did.

She briefly spotted a yellow dot among the hills to the west.

Linc pointed. "The clan's camp?"

"Yes. They circled their wagons there. The children and flocks . . . Dasanie was there; I don't know how he got loose."

199

"Probably intentional. The women wouldn't let him get away by accident."

"You really think so?"

He nodded. "If you don't mind, let's spend the night with them. Tell the elder about Neeskah and Dasanie. Maybe buy some corn and beans, since they aren't traveling far after all. I'm low on grub."

"I don't mind." And she didn't. Doli would continue north probably. She wanted to join relatives, Linc said. And neither did she feel jealous about Doli. Doli was a good woman. But Linc had made his choice just as she had made hers.

Linc rambled on, uncharacteristically loquacious. "The way I see it, Yale already has more culture than it can possibly stand. Now farm country, those are the people who need all the culture they can get. And I don't mean the phony kind. I mean a real enthusiasm for poetry and reading and philosophy and all that. You know, I almost forgot what new-mown hay smells like, and wheat fields after the rain."

Naomi sighed happily. "And the dairy shed at milking time. And when they're putting molasses in the cow feed on a warm day. And while you're milking, the cat just sits there, so you squirt a stream of milk right in its mouth and then it spends the next ten minutes licking all the milk off its fur from where you missed a little."

His voice purred. "And a sow or two to red up table scraps, with nine little piggies fighting to be first in the chowline."

She snuggled deep against him, deliciously content, as the past and the future melted together. "But first of all—God."

"Yeah. I may be ready for that too."

"If we marry, Linc, you're stuck with me forever, you know."

"The only way to do it."

"I really miss my father's farm, you know that?"

His was the voice of a happy man. "You're gonna love Alberta."

ABOUT THE AUTHOR

SANDY DENGLER, who spent several years in both Ohio and Arizona, now lives on the flank of a volcano, albeit a slumbering one—Mount Rainier—in Ashford, Washington. Because her husband is a ranger, her two teen-aged daughters have grown up in national parks.

Sandy is a prolific writer and observer of life, whose enthusiasm for history has been honed by helping with historical interpretation in several different parks. She has thereby learned in passing that: 1) bustles are a nuisance, but hoopskirts are worse; and 2) sidesaddles aren't all that bad—once you get used to them!

A Letter To Our Readers

Dear Reader:

Pioneering is an exhilarating experience, filled with opportunities for exploring new frontiers. The Zondervan Corporation is proud to be the first major publisher to launch a series of inspirational romances designed to inspire and uplift as well as to provide wholesome entertainment. In order that we might better contribute to your reading enjoyment, we would appreciate your taking a few minutes to respond to the following questions and return to:

Anne Severance, Editor
Serenade/Saga Books
749 Templeton Drive
Nashville, Tennessee 37205

1. Did you enjoy reading SUMMER SNOW?

   ☐ Very much. I would like to see more books by this author!
   ☐ Moderately
   ☐ I would have enjoyed it more if _____

2. Where did you purchase this book? _____

3. What influenced your decision to purchase this book?

   ☐ Cover   ☐ Back cover copy
   ☐ Title   ☐ Friends
   ☐ Publicity   ☐ Other _____

4. Please rate the following elements (from 1 to 10):

☐ heroine ☐ Plot
☐ Hero ☐ Inspirational theme
☐ Setting ☐ Secondary characters

5. Which settings do you prefer?

_____   _____

_____   _____

6. What are some inspirational themes you would like to see treated in future Serenade books?

_____   _____

_____   _____

7. Would you be interested in reading other Serenade/Serenata or Serenade/Saga Books?

☐ Very interested
☐ Moderately interested
☐ Not interested

8. Please indicate your age range:

☐ Under 18 ☐ 25–34 ☐ 46–55
☐ 18–24 ☐ 35–45 ☐ Over 55

9. Would you be interested in a Serenade book club? If so, please give us your name and address:

Name _____

Occupation _____

Address _____

City _____ State _____ Zip _____

Serenade Saga Books are inspirational romances in historical settings, designed to bring you a joyful, heart-lifting reading experience.

Serenade Saga books available in your local book store:

1 SUMMER SNOW, Sandy Dengler
2 CALL HER BLESSED, Jeanette Gilge
3 INA, Karen Baker Kletzing
4 JULIANA OF CLOVER HILL,
      Brenda Knight Graham
5 SONG OF THE NEREIDS, Sandy Dengler
6 ANNA'S ROCKING CHAIR, Elaine Watson